DESERT SURGEON

Disillusioned after a broken engagement and determined to devote herself to nursing, Harriet travelled East to Tehran. Working as a Sister in a hospital close to the deserts of Iran would, she thought, help her to recover more quickly. She certainly didn't anticipate that before long three men would be disturbing her planned existence, and that one of them would have such a shattering effect on her.

Books by Marjorie Curtis
in the Linford Romance Library:

DOCTOR'S REQUEST

MARJORIE CURTIS

DESERT SURGEON

Complete and Unabridged

LINFORD
Leicester

First published in Great Britain in 1976 by
Robert Hale Limited
London

First Linford Edition
published 1996
by arrangement with
Robert Hale Limited
London

British Library CIP Data

Curtis, Marjorie
    Desert surgeon.—Large print ed.—
    Linford romance library
    1. English fiction—20th century
    2. Large type books
    I. Title
    823.9'14 [F]

    ISBN 0–7089–7959–9

Published by
F. A. Thorpe (Publishing) Ltd.
Anstey, Leicestershire

Set by Words & Graphics Ltd.
Anstey, Leicestershire
Printed and bound in Great Britain by
T. J. Press (Padstow) Ltd., Padstow, Cornwall

This book is printed on acid-free paper

1

KEANE FORD BROWN left the dining-room and walked in a relaxed manner into the adjoining lounge. He was a handsome, dark-haired man with an air of confidence that many of his colleagues envied. Glancing idly at the occupants he noticed Doctor Maddox, one of his fellow countrymen, and chose an armchair next to him.

Stanley Maddox raised his head from the Tehran Journal he had been reading. "Had a busy morning?" he asked politely.

Keane shook his head. "No. I had a few hours off. Heavy day tomorrow though. I shall be in Theatre without a break."

"Who is assisting you this time?"

"The Frenchman, Paul Devaux."

"He's pretty good so I've been told."

1

Keane smiled. "It's easy in this hospital. Rather different from St Thomas'. I've never operated in such a well-equipped hospital."

"The technicians are first class also as you've probably noticed. After a time we take it all for granted. How long have you been here now?"

"About three months."

Stan's rugged face creased into a smile and his hazel eyes became slightly wistful. "I've been in Tehran a year and am looking forward to my vacation."

"Going home or are you intending to explore Iran's deserts?"

"You serious?" Stan grinned. "Mind you Tehran can be fascinating. Trouble is it wears off. There's nowhere quite like Britain."

Keane said carelessly, "Our European colleagues say the same about their own countries."

"I dare say. I haven't regretted coming and I intend to return. It's been a useful experience meeting and working with doctors from all over the world. There's a sprinkling from many countries."

"I've noticed that they are Scandinavian and European mostly. I thought the language problem might be a hindrance but so far I've not had any difficulty in making myself understood."

"Most of them speak English. French gets one by and a little German helps. It's the patients I've found puzzling." Doctor Maddox paused then went on, "The majority of them speak some kind of pidgin German or Farsi the official language."

Keane nodded. "Persian is not unlike Latin. It amazes me how the nurses cope."

"Most of them come from Tehran."

Keane asked casually, "What kind of woman is Sister Lawford?"

"Harriet?" Doctor Maddox looked startled then doubtful, "Haven't you met her?"

"Only officially in Theatre."

"She's marvellous; a first rate nurse."

"I didn't mean that. Obviously she's

good otherwise she wouldn't be here. What's her background like?"

Stan gazed at him in a puzzled fashion. "Average," he said reluctantly.

Keane's grey eyes were faintly exasperated. "It's rather like prising information from an oyster! You know more than that, surely?"

"Why do you want to know?"

"I haven't got designs on her! I'm curious that's all. I was strolling towards the less fashionable quarters of Tehran this morning when I noticed her."

"It would be difficult not to with that gold hair and lissom figure. What was she up to? Evidently she was engaged in something which alarmed you."

"She was talking to a young man; a disreputable ruffian. That's the only way I can describe him. He was practically in rags, was unshaven and had greasy black hair."

"Was he molesting her?"

"If he had been I would have gone to her assistance. No, it was quite the contrary. She was actually smiling and

4

laughing at him, speaking to him as if she knew him."

Doctor Maddox frowned. "I wish she wouldn't roam about the city on her own. It's very dangerous for young women to be unescorted. English girls are so careless."

"Now you know why I asked about her background. I wasn't being snobbish. I really felt concerned about the girl."

Stan nodded his fair head. "I would have been the same. I first met her at St Aubyn's. I was Senior Medical Officer and she was a Staff Nurse then and well liked. She was engaged to be married." He broke off and frowned. "I had forgotten all this. I wish you hadn't asked me."

"Because you were interested in her yourself?" Keane asked shrewdly.

"Very much so. I wasn't the only one. She left a trail of broken hearts behind. But she was so intent on this guy she was engaged to no one else had a chance."

"What happened?"

"She left and I didn't see her for a couple of months. Then one day she came back, cool as cucumber as I recall. She didn't believe in wearing her heart on her sleeve. It was some time before I ascertained the facts. Apparently her fiancé had cried off two days before the wedding. All the arrangements had to be cancelled."

"Why didn't she go to another hospital? There was no need for her to rub salt in the wound. Everyone must have known."

"That's Harriet for you; proud and redoubtable almost to the point of destruction. I tell you, Keane, she's quite some woman! I had applied for a transfer so I didn't see her again until we met here."

"Did you try to contact her?"

"Yes, I did. I had been at St Thomas' about six months when I heard that she had suffered another tragedy. Both her parents had been killed in an air crash. I rang St Aubyn's right away but was told she had been given sick leave and she had gone abroad for a spell."

"Tragic!" Keane exclaimed. "Yet none of what you have told me throws any light on the incident this morning."

Stan smiled. "If you want to know the reason for that you will have to ask her yourself but don't be surprised if she puts you in your place!"

Doctor Maddox smiled to himself as his colleague left him and strolled from the lounge. He's in for a jolt, he thought with amusement. It won't be as easy as he thinks. Harriet has a way of evading the issue. She won't tell anyone more than she wants them to know. She's hidden herself behind a wall, too thick to penetrate. Keane has a reputation of being irresistible to women. It will be interesting to see how he progresses with Harriet. If he gets very far he's a better man than I am.

Harriet took her time returning to the hospital. She was on night duty and had many hours to kill before she had to report back. It was a beautiful June day with hot sunshine and she felt disinclined to go indoors until she really had to.

She had a sandwich and vodka in an Armenian eating-house completely oblivious of the slanting glances from Persian and Arab men. In Tehran most of the population wore western dress and Harriet had become used to walking amongst them freely, ignoring the fact that quite a few of the women covered half their faces with the traditional chador, an ample, light veil crossed in front and knotted behind the neck. An Iranian nurse had told her they wore it as a symbol of respectability but she had no desire to wear one herself although she might have been less noticeable and safer with one. There had been one or two occasions when she had to escape swiftly from inquisitive eyes and hands.

That she had come to no harm was mainly due to her manner. Her voice was quiet yet had a ring of authority

8

in the soft tones and her blue eyes could look coldly on any who tried to molest her.

When she had arrived six months ago she had been a little disappointed because the capital was not as oriental as she had expected it to be. But now she was beginning to get the feel of it, finding remnants of its exciting past in the modern sophisticated city dominated by the snowcapped Elburz mountains.

That morning she had wandered through alleys bordered with *chinar* trees where streams of clear mountain water trickled at the foot of brick walls enclosing flower gardens and houses. She had watched the water-carrier sprinkling water on the dusty trees and had recalled Spanish women keeping the dust down in their narrow streets with their watering cans.

After lunch she strolled into the gardens of the Palace but did not venture inside the ceremonial residence. There was so much to see in Tehran outside the museums and famous buildings and with the sun shining she could not be tempted to leave it.

The Bazaar Harriet visited last of all fearing that she might be weak enough to buy something and have to carry it about with her all day. But this time she could see nothing she could afford and reluctantly began to make her way back to the hospital. She had bought nuts and grapes for some of the patients in the public ward and after she had washed and tidied herself she went there first.

The annex or free clinic as it was sometimes called lay well back from the imposing, modern building. Most of the sick came from hovels which sprang up continually as desert wanderers set up home in the outskirts of the city. The authorities could not keep pace with them for as fast as they pulled down the temporary houses more wanderers arrived and erected their hovels.

Harriet felt extremely sorry for these unfortunates and in an unassuming way did what she could for them. She found them very eager to be friendly and pathetically grateful to the nurses.

They were all women in the ward she entered and those who were not seriously ill welcomed her with bright smiles and exclamations of pleasure. She distributed the nuts and fruit leaving a young woman who was watching her eagerly until the last. Her brown skin and long black hair showed up the whiteness of the linen and pillow-slips.

Harriet smiled at her as she approached the bed. "How are you today, Nafisa? Are you doing your exercises and eating your meals?"

"*Naleh*, Sister."

"That's good! You will be able to leave here very soon."

The young woman's dark eyes regarded her wistfully "I don't want to leave without my baby."

Harriet looked at her thoughtfully. The Sister in charge would expect Nafisa to leave when she was well enough with or without her infant. Every bed was needed for there was a long waiting list. But this woman did not live in the city. She belonged to a tribe of Nomads who wandered in the deserts south and west of Tehran. Nafisa had been in labour when she was brought in. It had been a difficult birth. Fortunately for Nafisa, her husband had become frightened thinking that she was going to die and had travelled to the city carrying his wife on a mule. If he had delayed Nafisa and her baby would not have survived. The baby was premature and was still in an oxygen tent and being fed intravenously.

"I will see what I can do," Harriet said giving her an encouraging smile. "Meanwhile you do your best to improve. Eat the nuts and grapes and try to keep cheerful."

"*Techekour*," Nafisa's black eyes filled with tears. "You are so good to me. I shall never forget you."

"Do cheer up! Everything is going to be all right." Harriet pressed her hand gently. "I have a surprise for you. When I was out this morning I saw your husband."

"You did!" Nafisa brushed her tears away. "How is he? Is he well?" she asked eagerly.

"He was in high spirits. When I told him how quickly you were progressing he laughed and joked. He apologized for not coming to see you. He wanted to but he was too far away."

"Why didn't he come this morning?"

"He thought he might not be allowed to see you. Also he had some business to attend to and someone was waiting for him."

Nafisa sighed. "It is always so. Before I came to Tehran I did not think our ways were strange. But now I have seen how the city men treat their wives. They are so attentive! They always visit them and bring flowers and sweets."

Harriet laid her hand gently on the girl's shoulder. "It's never wise to compare, my dear. Life is more difficult for your husband. He's very worried about you and delighted about the baby. Why do you think he took the trouble to bring you here? He loved you and thought you would be safer in hospital."

The girl's eyes brightened. "That is true, yes. The old women did not want him to come. They were angry with him."

"You see, there's nothing to worry about! Once your baby has started on normal feeding you will be able to take him with you."

Harriet paused to chat with two of the nurses for a few minutes then walked across to the nurses' block and took the lift up to her quarters. She rested on her bed for an hour then took a bath and put on her uniform. She met Sister Zeid on her way to the dining-room and they sat down together.

Adina Zeid had received her training in the hospital so she had been there a few years. She was an attractive dark-haired young woman with slanting oriental eyes. She had lived in Tehran all her life so Harriet found her knowledge of the city very useful.

"Are you going on duty or coming off?" Harriet asked.

Adina yawned. "Can't you tell? I've just finished. After I've eaten I'm going to bed. There is a full Theatre day tomorrow and I shall need all my wits to carry me through. I'm assisting one of your countrymen, Mr Ford Brown."

Harriet pulled a face. "Enough said! I had a session with him a few weeks ago. You will find him terribly abrupt."

"He's a bit scaring, I must admit. He expects us all to be quicker than he is. So far I've escaped without much comment but I've only assisted at minor ops."

"I wonder what made him come to Tehran," Harriet remarked idly.

"Money and a thirst for glory in new fields." Adina laughed. "I've never seen such an unfathomable man. His eyes are cooler than a Scandinavian."

"He's got a determined jaw. I

wouldn't care to have an argument with him. So far I've managed to keep out of his way. I usually find I get on well with the surgeons and doctors I have to work with. I wouldn't like to spoil that achievement."

"I've noticed you keep them at a professional level." Adina glanced at her curiously. "Aren't you attracted to any of them?"

"No. I never see them other than as doctors." Harriet sighed. "I can't afford to be involved. I want to enjoy the time I spend in Iran."

"Some would say you would enjoy it more. You are different from the rest of us. Most of the nurses can't wait to find an escort. Night life in Tehran can be so exciting."

Harried smiled. "My wings have been singed. Don't worry about me. I've felt quite happy since I've been here. I'm so grateful for the experience gained. It's been very worthwhile."

"That's all right I suppose if you intend to be a career woman. It wouldn't be enough for me."

Harriet stared at her with sadness in her blue eyes. "I thought so too, once," she said then she smiled. "Now I live each day as it comes without considering the future. That philosophy has carried me through so far. I hope it will continue to do so."

Adina said apologetically "I'm sorry, Harriet. I can guess that some man has hurt you. I wouldn't have spoken as I did if I had known."

"It doesn't matter any longer. I haven't thought about him for a year now. If things had turned out differently I would be married, living in a house of my own and oblivious of this hospital." She gazed thoughtfully at her friend. "I don't regret what happened. I can see now there are other things in life just as worthwhile."

"You will meet someone else," Adina said quietly.

"Maybe. It's not important. I'm enjoying being my own mistress making my own decisions and spending my money instead of saving it," Harriet said flippantly.

Adina laughed as she got up to leave the dining-room. "That's not difficult! I can never save although I ought to."

I ought to be well used to night duty by now, Harriet reflected as she walked into the elevator and pressed the button for the fourth floor. But I never feel as easy and confident as I do in the daytime. Everything seems unreal at night. It will be a great relief to return to days. It's just a natural reaction I suppose. We are meant to sleep at night.

As she was a few minutes early she stopped at the intensive care unit on her way along the corridor. All was quiet in the semi-darkened room and the Swedish nurse nodded and smiled at her as she went to start the four-hourly pulse checks. There were three patients in the room, all under sedation. One, a girl of twenty, had recently undergone a major heart operation and Harriet went over to her bed and examined her critically.

"Zenda has recovered remarkably well," she said quietly after she had looked at her chart. "Has Mr Ford Brown been in to see her recently?"

"Yes, just a few minutes ago. He seemed pleased."

"He would be. I believe he was ready to operate again. She's a pretty girl, isn't she?"

"Yes, she is, Sister. She comes from Isfahan."

Harriet looked surprised. "I wonder why they sent her here? They have excellent hospitals there."

The Swedish nurse smiled. "Mr Ford Brown's fame is spreading. Her father heard about him and insisted she be sent here. There was an article in the newspaper about our heart surgeon. I expect he saw it."

"I don't really know very much about him. Evidently he is good. Being on night duty one tends to overlook the surgeons."

"Yes, Sister. When I've been on

nights I've noticed I do forget there are other doctors and nurses. We live in a world apart."

Harriet went out quietly and continued up the corridor. Private cubicles were either side for patients wishing to have a room to themselves but she did not enter these making her way towards the large ward at the end.

She noticed that the door of Sister's office was wide open and went to investigate for it was unusual. Expecting to find it empty she received a shock when she saw Mr Ford Brown sitting in the chair behind the desk. Some of the drawers of the filing cabinet were half open and the room looked very disordered.

On hearing her approach he raised his head and said abruptly, "Good evening, Sister. You can come in. I'm nearly finished."

Harriet hesitated. "I ought to speak to Sister Van Heese first," she said doubtfully.

"No need. She's gone. She's left her

case notes there for you. She wanted to get off early so I offered to wait for you."

"I see."

"Why the frown? I'm perfectly capable of responding to any emergency which might arise."

She smiled. "I imagine you are."

"I've been making use of my time by looking up the case histories of future patients who may need surgery."

"Zenda Payvar is making a remarkable recovery. I have just been in to see her."

"That's why you are late."

Harriet glanced at her fob watch. "Correction, Sir. I am still a few minutes early."

He said shortly, "Then my watch must be slow."

Harriet smiled. "Fast, Sir."

"Yes, yes. What does it matter. There's no need to make a fuss over a few minutes." He leaned back in his chair. "Heart surgery is ninety per cent safer than it used to be. Did you know that?" When she nodded he went on, "Zenda will be out of the intensive care unit in a couple of days."

"Her father will be delighted. He was so anxious about her."

"You know him?"

"I try to meet close relatives of the patients whenever I can."

Keane stared at her with cool smoke-grey eyes. "Is that what you were doing today?"

She was startled but quickly hid her reaction and drew herself up stiffly. "I'm not sure what you are referring to," she said evenly.

"I noticed you on the outskirts of the city. It was a most unsuitable neighbourhood for you to be in. You were accosted by a man who looked like a gypsy. I would have intervened but you seemed to be handling the situation well enough. No doubt you have experienced something of the kind before. But it was foolish to allow goodwill to blind your prudence. Don't you agree?"

Behind her polite smile anger quickened. How dare he spy on her she fumed. She hadn't been in uniform. She could please herself what she did in her free time. She did not even know Ford Brown. The nerve of him to criticize her movements!

With an immense effort she swallowed her annoyance and replied coldly, "There was no danger. I had met the man before. He is the husband of Nafisa. She's in the annex waiting to be discharged."

"Yes, she would be in there." The sneer in his voice faded before the sudden blaze of her blue eyes. Hyacinth blue, a beautiful colour, he reflected, unaccountably shaken by the striking contrast of golden hair and the vivid blue of her eyes.

"Yousaf was extremely polite," Harriet remarked coolly. "Because he is a Nomad doesn't necessarily mean that he is as ill-mannered as some of my countrymen."

Wow! That she had meant himself

was unmistakable for she had stared directly into his eyes. Keane sat back and straightened in his chair. Sister Lawford could drive a punch home when she had a mind to, he thought wryly. But what an interesting combination she was! At first sight, a quiet gentle person. Yet she could utter softly spoken words that could sting. All the time he had been talking to her he had been aware of something held in reserve. Contempt and an inner core of hardness, perhaps? She has been badly hurt, he mused. That would account for it or some of it.

Aware that she was staring at him curiously he said smoothly, "I apologize. My remark was thoughtless and in bad taste. But to get back to what we were talking about I still stick to my opinion. This isn't my first stay in foreign countries. It's only too easy to become involved in unpleasant incidents. You can't see yourself or realize the effect you have. In the east blondes are so noticeable. You forget

24

that you are not as safe here as you would be in your own country."

"I've not noticed anything different," she said carelessly. "I don't go out of my way to attract attention. There is just as much danger in our cities if you look for it."

"I'm not saying it's anything you do. I was suggesting that you be more careful," he said mildly.

Her blue eyes twinkled. "You think I ought to hide myself behind a chador?"

He regarded her gravely. "It wouldn't be such a bad idea."

She laughed disbelievingly. "Are you sure you're not an Arab in outlook! Westerners prefer their women without a veil."

"You know very well what I mean. I was giving you some sensible advice."

She stared at him thoughtfully,. "Why me? Or do you make a habit of advising women."

"This conversation is becoming foolish." He shrugged his broad shoulders and looked at her through narrowed eyes. "Doctor Maddox said you would be difficult."

Pink colour stained her cheeks. "You have been discussing me with Stan Maddox?"

He gave her a cool indifferent glance. "I'm fairly new here. I recognized you this morning and was puzzled at your behaviour. Surely it was perfectly natural to enquire about you?"

She was silent for a minute or two trying to put herself in his place before she made some regrettable reply. She did not want to be unfair and some men were sincere. Perhaps he really had been concerned. Yousaf had looked dirty and rough; not a fit companion for a young white woman. At the time Harriet had not taken much notice for she understood after listening to Nafisa how difficult it was to keep themselves clean in the desert. Water was only used for drinking, rarely for washing. It was too scarce and precious. Also they were so poor that new clothes were quite beyond them.

"Have you gone into a trance, Sister?"

Harriet started rather guiltily. "I'm sorry. I was trying to see it through your eyes. I think I've been a little unfair."

"That's very generous of you."

She looked at him quickly not sure whether he was mocking her then asked cautiously, "Did Doctor Maddox tell you we used to work together?"

"Yes. He gave me a brief description of your life at St Aubyn's. Why? Does it distress you?"

"A little. No one cares to have their private life discussed. Stan ought not to have told you."

"I thought you came out of it rather well," he replied with a faint smile.

He did not see the sudden compression of her lips or the shadow of pain in her blue eyes for she turned away to close one of the filing cabinets.

"Can I find some of the record cards for you?" she asked.

"No need. I've finished. Make a note

of these, will you? I'm going to take them with me."

Harriet wrote the names down on her pad, tore off the sheet and dropped it inside the top drawer of the cabinet. Then methodically she began to file the others away.

"Your Junior can do that, surely!" he remarked with a frown.

"It will only take a second. I prefer to have everything in order in case we have a sudden emergency."

"I'm not on call, thank goodness!"

Harriet smiled sympathetically. "You will make up for it tomorrow."

He raised thick, dark eyebrows. "You know I'm in Theatre for most of the day?"

"Sister Zeid told me. I hope it goes smoothly."

"It ought to. There's only one tricky case. The man's had one major operation. I would feel happier if I had performed it."

"I can understand that. Will it be a long undertaking?"

He smiled. "I'm not sure I approve of that word. At a guess I would say eight or nine hours. Heart surgery can't be hurried although as you know we work as quickly as we can providing it is safe."

Harriet gazed at him curiously. "Most of the heart specialists I've known have been much older men," she said then felt slightly apprehensive because of her temerity.

He looked rather amused. "I'm thirty-two and not at the top yet."

"My remark wasn't any reflection on your skill," she said quickly.

His grey eyes glinted like cold steel. "I trust not! Criticism I expect from my superiors not the nursing staff. They would be well advised to keep to matters they can understand."

She became instantly aware that he was very touchy about his skill as a surgeon. The sudden change in his manner was like a douche of icy water. Seeing his implacable face and forbidding jaw Harriet realized she had stepped on sacred ground. With her past experience she ought to have known better. It was perfectly correct for a superior to make the running but a nurse always had to curb her curiosity and enthusiasm. He had probed into her personal life but she was not permitted to touch on his.

Something of the nature of her thoughts must have transferred itself to him for his expression lightened and he broke the sudden constraint between them.

"I've finished now. Have a pleasant night Sister. Thank you for assisting me."

When he had gone she sat down for a few minutes to give herself time to recover. Something had occurred which alarmed her in a vague way. Her protective wall was no longer foolproof. She had been aware of him as a man as well as a colleague. At moments his lance-like remarks had thrust home piercing her defences. She felt chastened and was annoyed with herself for allowing him to disrupt her serenity, for she had fought hard and long to gain it. Yet he had not been conscious of storming her citadel. She was quite certain of that. He had been carelessly friendly, critical and reproving even at times surprisingly comforting.

She smiled wryly. What nonsense I'm indulging in! He's a man who has become successful too swiftly. He's arrogant and proud and assumes he has the right to dictate to me. I shall disregard his warnings and do as I please. I can't ignore him for I may have to work with him. But one thing I do know. I shall never let him disturb me again.

2

HARRIET did not see Mr Ford Brown for over a week. Night duty prevented her from attending the socials held twice weekly for the staff. She was beginning to feel cut off from everyone except the few she came in contact with when on duty and she was pleased when she was changed back to days.

She was to be in charge of Men's Medical Ward, not one some sisters liked for patients tended to stay longer than in the Surgical Ward. But Harriet did not mind. She would have a capable team of nurses and she would not have to assist in Theatre unless there was an emergency or she was asked for particularly. She did not think that was likely and there would be less chance of running into Ford Brown. She was not eager to see that gentleman again.

The first morning on Men's Medical passed smoothly and she went for a stroll after lunch, timing herself to return a few minutes before she was due back. As she was about to mount the steps leading to the Staff entrance, a tall man wearing riding breeches and a white shirt open at the neck came through the swinging glass doors. Harriet, stared at him in slight astonishment for he looked so different from the last time she had encountered him. Today Keane seemed young and carefree, handsome in a dashing kind of way; one so foreign to the serious minded surgeon who had questioned and advised her.

"Good morning, Sister!" There was a glint in his grey eyes which mocked her. "Pity you can't join me. It's a marvellous day for riding."

"I've never been very interested in it," she replied.

"Pity! You have the figure for it."

She smiled faintly. "I imagine you

have to have more than that. Where do you go?"

"The Country Club. One of my patients recommended me."

"You were lucky. I believe it's exclusive."

Keane nodded his head then gave her a keen look. "I heard you are on day duty now. Perhaps we shall see you more often. There's a social tonight in case you have forgotten."

"Yes. I may go. It will make a change."

He eyed her critically. "You ought to mix with people more. It's not good for you to be on your own so much."

She smiled. "I see plenty of people every day."

"On duty, yes. That's not what I meant. How you do twist everything! I shall see you tonight then." Nodding a dismissal he strode purposefully away.

Harriet saw him go with a faint frown marring her smooth forehead. She was conscious of a ruffled resentment as if he had deliberately stirred her complacency into action. I do wish Stan hadn't told him of my broken engagement, she thought crossly. I suppose he feels he has to be pleasant to me. I don't want his sympathy or his well meaning advice. I've won my battle and I dislike being pitied.

She gave a sudden short laugh. He's only one of the surgeons she told herself in amusement. He's not important to me. Why should I care what he thinks or does. It might be quite funny if he persists in going out of his way to be kind. I shall know the reason why but others won't. It's sure to be misinterpreted. The grape-vine is avid for gossip whether true or false.

Sister Zeid stopped to chat with her as she waited for the lift. A fair-haired pretty girl hurried past them on her way to the exit. Harriet glanced at her curiously for she was dressed in riding kit and looked very trim and attractive.

Adina smiled and whispered, "She's going to meet Ford Brown. They go riding together. No one is supposed to know but I've seen them meeting outside the hospital."

"Who is she?" Harriet asked.

"An Austrian nurse. She's been assisting Ford Brown in Theatre."

"Rather her than me!" Harriet exclaimed.

"He doesn't waste much time, does he? So far he's dated most of the nicest looking females in the hospital."

Harriet chuckled. "How come we've escaped? Perhaps he likes variety and believes there's safety in numbers."

"I'm not available. My young man wouldn't approve."

Harriet stared at her. "I didn't know you were serious about anyone."

"It's not official yet but my parents like him. He's half Jewish just as we are."

"I'm so pleased for you," Harriet said sincerely. "Here's the lift. I ought to go. I will see you at dinner."

One or two emergencies came in and Harriet was too occupied to think of anything but what was happening on her ward. Doctor Maddox came in to see his patients and Harriet accompanied him on his round.

"I shall miss you when you leave for your vacation," she remarked after he had examined a man who was suffering from a bout of malaria. It was an unusual case for malaria was almost extinct in Iran but the man had recently arrived from North Africa and had been taken ill in his hotel.

"I wish I could believe that," Doctor Maddox replied. "I suppose it would be foolish of me to try again."

"To be honest, it would," Harriet said seriously. "I value your friendship, Stan. It will be a very long time before I become really interested in a man."

He smiled. "It's too difficult to believe you mean that."

"You will have to for I'm serious. I'm happier now than I've been for a long time. So I'm not encouraging pain and disillusionment again."

"It needn't be like that with the right man."

"How would I know? I couldn't face the uncertainty. Even the right man could make problems. No, I shall remain independent."

Doctor Maddox stared at her thoughtfully. "The best laid plans come unstuck Harriet. You are in for a shock. Emotions can't be regulated scientifically."

"Mine can." She chuckled. "It will take an earthquake to make me change."

Stan smiled. "That's probably what it will feel like. It's unwise to believe you are immune. However I ought to feel thankful for small mercies. All the time you are free there's some hope for me."

Harriet shook her head. "If there had been anything between us it would have shown itself before now. We have known each other too long. If you were sensible you would agree with me."

He sighed. "Oh, I do. I resigned

myself long ago. But I would like to see you happy, Harriet. Your contentment won't last, I'm sure you are aware of that."

"Perhaps. But I need an interim period. My bruises don't show but they are there." She moved towards the door. "Would you take a look at Ali Mifsud before you go? He had a very bad night. The drugs haven't quietened him at all; quite the reverse."

"Yes. I was half afraid of that. We will put him on something milder. That's the trouble with some of these wonder drugs. They can kill or cure. I guess they will never finish experimenting. It would be so much easier if all humans had the same reactions."

Harriet smiled. "If it was that easy you would be grumbling at the boredom of your task."

Chatting amicably as if to an equal Doctor Maddox walked with Harriet along the corridor to the private room of Ali Mifsud. It was one of the things that she appreciated. Stan never talked down to her as so many specialists did. He recognized her intelligence and knew she was an accomplished Sister and treated her with the respect she deserved.

By the end of the day Harriet was in two minds whether to go to the social. She was feeling tired, not unusual the first day a nurse came off nights. And the new ward had proved rather exacting. She had had to learn swiftly the ailments of her patients and deal diplomatically with nurses she had not seen before.

Eager to get out of her uniform she went to her room as soon as she had finished dinner. She took a shower, put on a dressing-gown and re-set her hair. Then selecting a book which had been recommended to her she curled up in an armchair to relax for awhile. But she became so engrossed that she forgot about the social until Adina knocked on her door.

"You aren't ready!" Sister Zeid

exclaimed in a disappointed voice. "Have you decided not to come?"

Harriet smiled apologetically. "I'm sorry. You go without me. I will make you late."

"That doesn't matter. Please come. I always enjoy your company so much. I've missed you since you've been on nights."

"I have to do my face and hair."

Adina chuckled "That won't take long. You never use much make-up."

"I never have the time and when I do I feel too lazy. But a little mascara and lipstick is needed in the evening."

"Wear your blue dress," Adina said. "It makes your eyes look marvellous."

"It's not very up-to-date," Harriet replied doubtfully. "Your dress looks as if it cost a month's salary."

"Not quite!" Adina glanced down at her tan coloured dress with white trimmings and smiled. "It was a birthday present from my parents. I couldn't afford to buy it."

"Are your parents wealthy?"

41

"Fairly. I'm very lucky. I have my own car and I'm nearly as independent as you western girls are. You will have to come home with me when we both have a free day at the same time. You will be surprised I think at the way we live."

"I've heard that in Tehran most of the middle classes live as Europeans do as regards houses and furniture."

"That's correct. My mother does not cover her face and she and my father wear western dress."

Harriet put down her comb and slipped her dress on. "I'm ready!" she said.

Adina laughed. "You have your slippers on."

"Oh dear! They are so comfortable." Harriet sighed as she opened her wardrobe and took out a pair of beige shoes. She stepped into them gingerly and then surveyed herself in the mirror tilting it so that she could see her feet. "They don't go very well," she muttered in a disgruntled voice.

"Don't worry. It will be so crowded no one will be able to see your feet."

"I remember! Last time I nearly ruined my white sandals. Some clumsy young technician walked all over them. I had to send them to be repaired."

"I hope they have some new records. It's becoming rather monotonous listening to the same ones."

"We can always play bridge or table tennis," Harriet said. "The get-togethers here are a vast improvement on my last hospital."

"The nurses' and doctors' quarters have only been built recently. When I started my training the staff used to live in the main block. Of course there were fewer staff and not so many patients. They hoped to attract foreign medical staff so the accommodation had to be modern and comfortable."

"It's certainly that. But having a fully equipped hospital would be enough to attract most doctors and surgeons." Harriet said. "I'm as ready as I shall ever be. Shall we go?"

Harriet soon forgot that she was tired. She knew quite a few of the doctors and technicians and as soon as she and Adina entered the room four young men left the bar to join them. Harriet had forgotten Ford Brown until she noticed him dancing with the Austrian nurse. They seemed engrossed with one another and after a few minutes Harriet turned her attention elsewhere.

After what Keane had said to her Harriet half expected him to come over and speak to her but beyond raising a hand when their eyes met he did not leave the Austrian girl's side. Harriet felt slightly disappointed but could not understand why. After all she did not know the man and had been annoyed with him for interfering with her private life.

Stan Maddox came in later and joined Harriet's group. Two of the young men had moved away to greet other friends but the two who remained seemed determined not to allow Doctor Maddox to dance too often with Harriet.

Altogether it was a very pleasant evening and both Adina and Harriet were pleased that they had gone. Keane left before they did taking his partner with him.

"Keane seems to fancy that fair-haired nurse," Stan remarked in an amused voice as he walked the two Sisters back to their block.

Adina laughed lightly. "Perhaps it's the other way round."

"He's a lucky man then. I believe she's fancy free and wealthy."

"I thought her dress had the stamp of Paris," Harriet said.

"She's a pleasant enough girl," Stan said carelessly. "Not in your class Harriet."

She laughed. "You are good for me. But you must admit you are prejudiced about English nurses. Adina is as good if not better than I am."

"Not yet," the girl said seriously. "I haven't had the benefit of your superior training but I am learning fast."

Harriet was scarcely paying attention to what she was saying for she was wondering why there seemed to be such a commotion all of a sudden. Technicians and doctors were tearing past them, running towards the main building.

"What's up?" Doctor Maddox asked one man who had stopped to pick up a note-book he had dropped.

"There's been a train accident. Many casualties so I've been told. We have to report to Casualty."

"I shall have to, go," Stan said. "I'm not on call but I might be needed."

Harriet glanced at Adina who nodded her head and then said quickly. "We will come with you.

"Get into your uniforms first!" Stan called out as he hurried away.

The two sisters went to their rooms and changed swiftly then joined the stream of nurses and doctors who were making their way to Casualty. After that they lost all sense of time and spent a hectic three hours tending one casualty after another. When all the serious cases had been sent to the wards or straight into Theatre for surgery Harriet and Adina decided to leave. Most of the minor cases were being dealt with and there was no point in hanging about getting in the Casualty Staff's way.

Harriet was moving towards the exit when a Sister using the house phone called from Theatre asking for Sister Lawford. An orderly passed on the message to Harriet but could not tell her why she was wanted.

Stan Maddox enlightened her as she went up in the lift with him.

"Its the badly injured man with the crushed chest. Ford Brown is going to operate. He especially asked for you and he wants me to stand by for after care." He shrugged his shoulders. "No one except Keane thinks he has a chance. The other surgeons shook their heads and suggested he allow the man to die painlessly."

Harriet said soberly, "If he is to die anyway and Keane thinks he may have a chance then he has to operate."

"I agree. I've seen Keane perform miracles before so I won't be too surprised if he does it again."

Harriet took over from the sister who had been assisting Keane with a calm efficiency which her early training had instilled in her. One swift glance at the patient was enough to tell her that Doctor Maddox had been right. It would be a miracle if Keane could save the man. After that she thought of nothing except obeying the surgeon's curt commands with a lightning response. The two nurses who had been a little nervous at assisting with such a serious case regained their confidence when they saw how competently their Sister was reacting to the rather frightening ordeal.

Harriet had been a little surprised to find junior nurses there but supposed they were the only two available. But she had assisted in Theatre so many times that it was second nature for her to know when to nod at the nurses and reprimand them quietly if they did something wrong whilst at the same time work in unison with the surgeon always a fraction ahead of his crisp commands for this or that instrument. Team work was vitally essential and all of them had to act swiftly and surely.

She left the nurses to clean up and was taking off her soiled gown when Keane came in. He had taken off his gloves and mask but was still wearing his long gown. Harriet frowned. It had all been rather unorthodox. Surely one of the nurses ought to have removed his gown.

"Can I untie you, sir?" she asked.

"If you would." His voice was husky with weariness for he had been in Theatre ever since the first casualty had been wheeled in.

"I'm sorry we have not been able to run our side of it as efficiently as it usually is. When there is only one surgeon we really need another nurse. Counting swabs takes up so much time. I could have been more useful holding down the retractors. It would have given you more freedom to use the forceps. There were so many bleeding points."

"I agree. I could have used another pair of hands. Unfortunately I couldn't get hold of another surgeon." Keane smiled. "I don't think we did so badly. Well done, Harriet. You did a splendid job."

She eased his gown off his shoulders and whisked it away before it fell to the floor. "I only assisted. You are the one who ought to be congratulated."

"It's too soon to do that. I was only the instrument. There was a chance. I had to take it. It's a humbling experience."

She looked at him curiously as he went to the washbasin and turned the taps. "Humbling? You look elated!"

He nodded as he soaped his hands.

"I feel pleased naturally. Yet sometimes having the power of life or death is frightening."

"That is what makes you great," Harriet said quietly. "You are inspired."

He smiled. "Hardly. It's having the knowledge and all the technical skill. All of you in that Theatre were vital to the success or failure of the operation. You can congratulate your staff for me."

"Thank you, sir. I'm going to the ward now and fix the drip. Are there any instructions for Sister on Men's Surgical?"

Keane frowned. "There's no need for you to do anything. Doctor Maddox has gone with the patient. He will know what to do. You look tired, Harriet. Go to bed and get some beauty sleep." He broke off then smiled faintly. "That was an unnecessary remark. Your beauty doesn't need reviving. It comes from within and glows even when you are weary."

She glanced at him in alarm thinking

that overwork had made him light-headed. But when she saw the twinkle in his grey eyes her cheeks coloured in confusion.

"Don't look so embarrassed! Haven't you ever had a compliment before?" he asked in an amused voice.

She chuckled. "Not after hours in Theatre. Good night, sir."

"Good night Harriet. Once again, thanks."

She returned to her quarters in an uneasy state of mind. Gone was the calm efficiency which had cloaked her throughout the operation. She had become used to words and glances of admiration from men but none had affected her as Keane's few words had done.

I'm tired, she told herself excusingly. And he's excited. Tomorrow all will be normal again. If I don't go to bed soon I won't be fit for the ward tomorrow. It's nearly four o'clock!

She was officially on duty at eight but knew that her night sister would be told she had been in Theatre for part of the night. She would not grumble if Harriet was a few minutes late. However one had to expect these emergencies. They happened in any hospital. And it had been very worthwhile.

A week passed and Harriet would soon be due for a long week-end off. She was aware of this but did not apply for it. She was enjoying running her ward and as there was no particular place she wanted to visit she decided to allow her leave to mount up.

The man badly hurt in the train crash was making progress slowly in the intensive care unit. Harriet visited him whenever she could spare a few minutes. Somehow she felt responsible although he was not her patient. She usually tried to go when she knew Ford Brown was occupied elsewhere. Since that night in Theatre she felt disinclined to meet him in off duty hours. Now that she was on a medical ward she did not have much to do with him.

She had deliberately missed the Social because she had thought he might be there. Her painful experience with Morris had left her vulnerable. Keane had touched some chord and it frightened her. She did not want to become fond of him. He had a strong attraction for her which she found disturbing so much that at times she disliked him for having that power over her.

I'm not going to be hurt again, she told herself fiercely. Keane is only being pleasant. He's still taking that Austrian nurse around with him. I think he finds me a little intriguing because I won't meet him half way.

She took refuge with Stan Maddox who understood how she felt. That it was not fair she knew but so strong was the feeling of self protection that she tended to overlook the interpretation he might make when she sought him out. But Doctor Maddox was well aware of her agitation for he had noticed that Harriet only gravitated towards him when Keane Ford Brown was on the scene.

"You won't be able to keep it up, Harriet," he said laughingly when they were strolling in the grounds of the hospital.

"Keep what up?" she asked idly with a glance at his homely square-jawed face.

"Avoiding Keane. He was looking for you just now."

"If it was anything important he would have come over."

"Not when I'm with you." He smiled. "It's okay. I understand. I don't mind being used."

She gave him a startled look. "Is it as obvious as that?"

"Only to me. You will have to surrender one day, Harriet. It's not as if you are still pining for Morris." he hesitated then asked cautiously, "Are you? Is that your problem?"

"No! I never think of him but then I've not seen him since he broke off our engagement."

"How would you feel if you met him again?"

"I don't know. That's hardly likely to happen so it's pointless talking about it."

"I know what I would do," Stan said belligerently. "I would pick a quarrel and thrash him until he cried for mercy."

Harriet laughed. "That would solve everything, naturally! Really, Stan, you ought to have more sense than that."

"It would make me feel better."

Harriet sighed. "It's nothing to do with you. Morris was certain he was acting for the best. Now when I reflect about it I think he was right although I don't approve of the way he left it until just before the day of the wedding."

"That was cruel."

"Yes. Stan, I'm not being fair to you. I think we ought not to spend our free time together."

"Keane will step into my shoes. You are aware of that, I suppose?"

"That's ridiculous! Anyway I don't

have to be friendly with him."

Doctor Maddox shrugged his shoulders. "You're a stubborn wench. You just won't see what is staring you in the face."

"You are wrong. And if you don't stop teasing me I shall go in. You are worse than a woman with your matchmaking."

"I shall have to go back," Stan said regretfully. "By the way, that little lady in the annex has been asking for you. She's due to be discharged and returns to her tribe tomorrow."

"Nafisa? Is she taking her baby with her?"

"Yes. You know I nearly came to blows with Sister Ruban over that. The young woman could have left a week ago but because you pleaded with me I cooked up some vague internal malfunction to keep her here. I'm certain Sister is suspicious. She's been very cool ever since and I've been expecting her to call in another doctor. If she does I shall never be able to show my face in the annex again."

"Oh, Stan, you're a darling!" Harriet chuckled. "I shall never forget how sympathetic you are. I might as well call in at the annex now. I still have a few more minutes before I go on duty."

Nafisa was dressed and sitting at a table in the centre of the ward. She looked completely recovered and her eyes shone when she saw Harriet coming towards her.

"It is good of you to come," the girl said gravely. "I know I have you to thank for remaining here."

Harriet sent a quick glance over her shoulder and sighed with relief when she saw that the nurses were at the other end of the ward. "Don't let Sister Ruban hear you say that!" She smiled. "We have to work together sometimes so you can understand it might be awkward."

"It would have broken my heart to have gone without my baby," Nafisa said softly. "Yousaf is coming for us tomorrow."

"Have you far to go?"

"I do not know where my people are now. It will be near a water-hole. If they have found somewhere to stay where the cattle can graze they will remain there for the summer. If not they will want to travel on. Yousaf does not want me to go far but it depends on the elders."

"Your baby has had a good start. Will you be able to look after him properly?"

Nafisa nodded. "I have learned much since I have been in here. And I will have help from my sisters and mother."

"How did you come to learn English?" Harriet asked curiously.

Nafisa smiled. "Some of my people are Qachquais and every winter we used to camp near Shiraz because it is so mild there. I went to school for a few weeks each year and was taught English."

"It's still surprising that you speak it so well. A few weeks a year is not long."

"When we travel in the desert we often encounter the Health Corps. I believe it's rather like your Red Cross. Some of their members spoke English so I became used to it. Also there is an Education Corps. We met some of them also."

"So you weren't cut off from the outside world all the time."

"No. Most of us have had some learning. But my people prefer to be free. That is why they do not settle in a city. But our way of life is gradually changing. The young people have different ideas and the lure of the cities is taking some of them away."

Harriet did not stay long for she had to return to duty. She noticed that Sister Ruban had been hovering near them curious about what they were talking about. And the woman gave Harriet an old fashioned look when she went over to speak to her before leaving the ward.

Harriet smiled to herself as she walked back to the main block. Sister

Ruban was a dragon, one of the old school. She disliked any interference with the running of her annex. Even the doctors had to be careful not to tread on her toes and in consequence she was not very popular. She was older than the other sisters and had been in Tehran three years. She did not approve of the constant flow of nurses, doctors and surgeons from Europe thinking that if they chose to come then they ought to stay much longer than they did.

There was a certain amount of truth in that. It was a little unsettling to have to keep adjusting to new faces and new methods. Harriet could understand how Sister Ruban felt but then perhaps she had no ties in France. Most of the foreign staff became homesick after a few months or a year and quite a few of them returned to their own countries as soon as their contracts had finished.

When Harriet met Adina that evening at dinner she mentioned Nafisa and her infant. The two young women had become very friendly ever since Harriet had spent an evening in Adina's home. She had been made extremely welcome by the Zeids who lived in a modern house north of Sha Reza boulevard. Harriet did not find it very different from western establishments except that the furniture tended to be massive and very ornate.

"Sometimes I feel so sorry for the women belonging to the Nomad tribes," Adina said. "Yet on occasions I envy them. Some of them are so gay and carefree."

Harriet nodded her head. "I know what you mean. They live only for the present. In cities people are so engrossed in earning enough to keep them in some kind of style that there is little time to enjoy themselves."

"I've been spoilt," Adina said. "I wouldn't last in the desert. I'm not tough enough. The desert people eat and live differently. They travel great distances under a scorching sun and there is no protection except at some of the water-holes. They wander between these using the meagre grazing land for their cattle. They have to put up with sand storms, minute amounts of water and sometimes fight off murderous bands of men who are even poorer than they are."

"Nafisa is such an intelligent girl. I became quite fond of her. It's a pity I won't see her again. I would like to know how she gets on. She said that some of her people belonged to the Qachquai tribe. They have been waiting for her before they moved on towards the Zagros mountains. Is that very far?"

"It depends whether they are moving west or south. I expect they will move towards Shiraz, that's south. If so it is a long way. Some Nomadic Tribes spend their winters on the plains around the Persian Gulf. The Qachquais were originally Turkish but they are scattered now. Perhaps it is a good thing for they were more interested in fighting amongst themselves than helping to improve conditions in Iran."

"I was surprised that they are so good," Harriet remarked.

Adina smiled. "You can't have seen the southern part of Tehran. The river is very muddy and provides the poor with their only supply of water. You can imagine what happens. They use it for everything! They live in hovels made of mud and straw and cook, eat and sleep in the same room."

"It sounds awful! At least Nafisa is spared that. She's not crowded on the edge of the city."

"Once Tehran was a large village on the caravan trails. Then merchants began to settle and very quickly it became an important city. Now it has western shops, movies, hotels and traffic jams plus an airport and railway station."

Harriet laughed. "I'm beginning to fear that I shall have to join your Health Corps if I want to see the real Iran. Don't be surprised if I vanish into the deserts one day in search of atmosphere and adventure!"

They were prophetic words spoken in jest. Harriet was to remember them in the days that lay ahead.

3

ONE afternoon two weeks later Harriet and Stan were playing tennis with Adina and Keane. As Keane was friendly with Stan and they had arranged the match between them Harriet had been unable to refuse. She felt a little annoyed with Stan but forgave him because she realized that she herself was at fault. She could not continue to avoid Keane who made a point of joining Adina, Stan and herself whenever he could. Harriet and Stan were used to playing together and were giving the other two a strenuous game.

"That's it!" Harriet called out when Adina failed to return her last service. "Game, set and match!"

"Sorry, Keane," Adina said breathlessly. "Harriet is just too swift for me."

Keane smiled. "You had the sun in your eyes."

As they left the court together Stan asked, "Have you time for a drink?"

"Only a soft drink for me," Adina said quickly. "I'm on duty soon."

They had been playing in the grounds of an hotel so they did not have far to go. When they reached the bar Harriet and Adina went to the cloak-room to change. Harriet put on light blue slacks and a white blouse; Adina zipped up a lime green dress leaving her legs bare.

"My mother would not approve," she remarked with a light laugh. "However I haven't far to go and I shall have to change again when I reach the hospital."

"In England we would walk through the streets in our tennis dresses," Harriet said. "I can imagine what Keane would say if I did so here!"

There was a sherry waiting for Harriet and an orange drink for Adina when they returned to the bar. Harriet caught Keane's grey glance appraising her and quickly looked away. Stan noticed and his lips curved with amusement but tactfully he made no comment. Harriet was looking extremely attractive and he did not blame Keane for being intrigued.

"There's a heated pool in this hotel," Keane told them after they had finished their drinks. "Anyone care for a swim?"

Harriet laughed. "I think we've had enough exercise. Anyway Adina can't come and we would have to go back for our costumes. We do swim occasionally. Adina and I go to the Sports Centre once a week."

"There's no lack of facilities for sport," Stan said. "Keane was able to play polo last week."

"Really?" Harriet glanced at Keane with interest. "That's an exciting game. Let us know next time you play and we will come and watch."

"That might be never." Keane smiled. "I just happened to be there when they were a man short. I can never rely on my free time so team work is out of the question."

68

"I shall have to leave you," Adina said regretfully. "Can I take your tennis gear back with me, Harriet?"

"That would be marvellous but can you manage it?"

Stan grinned. "Keane's can go in with mine. Adina and I will he able to carry all of it between us. Enjoy yourselves comrades."

Harriet glanced at him swiftly in alarm. She had been intending to go off on her own but now it seemed she was to have Keane for a companion. Stan winked at her before he and Adina left but she pretended not to notice. Then she saw that Keane was smiling and she was forced to smile back although she could cheerfully have kicked Stan on the ankles.

"Have you arranged to do anything?" Keane asked politely.

"Not really. I thought I might look at the shops," Harriet replied awkwardly.

"If you have no objection I will come with you. Have you visited a Mosque yet?"

Harriet shook her head. "I've been intending to but so far haven't had the opportunity."

"The King's Mosque is near here. You ought to visit it. It's an unforgettable experience."

"That means going through the Bazaar."

Keane smiled. "I won't let you be tempted to buy anything."

"You might find that difficult!" she replied laughingly.

Walking through the covered streets teeming with shoppers and sightseers they refrained from loitering in front of the merchants' tempting wares and elbowed their way through to the great courtyard.

Keane pulled a silk scarf from his neck and handed it to Harriet. "It might be wise to wear this," he said.

"Thanks." Harriet took it and tied it loosely over her hair. It was navy blue and contrasted with her golden hair making her eyes look even lovelier. "How's that?" she asked with a faint smile. "I didn't bring a mirror with me."

Keane's grey eyes twinkled. "I didn't think you liked compliments. You look entrancing."

She turned away feeling shy all of a sudden. It was the first time that they had been out together alone and she was terribly conscious of his nearness. But when she noticed that he was staring about him in an unconcerned way she soon recovered her composure.

The open court was flanked by bays or iwans with painted and glazed ablution basins. All the arcades and facades of the iwans were covered with beautiful yellow tiles which dazzled the eyes when the sun caught them. Gazing up at the golden, bulb dome and minarets facing towards Mecca, the towers that originally were used for the call to prayer, Harriet was conscious of a deep sense of serenity. Behind the arcades with their screen of metal lattice-work there was a peace which encompassed all who entered the temple. There were no seats only carpets on the floor of the domed sanctuary.

"Anyone who expects a Mosque to look like our places of worship are in for a disappointment," Keane remarked after they had returned to the courtyard and put on their shoes which they had slipped off. "Mosques are often assembly halls for religious colleges, sometimes even a court of justice."

"A meeting place! It is a very practical solution bringing material and spiritual things together. Perhaps they are right. The Mosque is their focal centre. I'm afraid our churches are not."

"Do you feel like a climb?" Keane asked.

"To the top of one of the minarets? No, I couldn't, not today."

"We will find a tea-room then. I'm sure you would enjoy some French or German pastries."

"I would like some tea or coffee," she confessed. "The sun has made me thirsty. I believe there's a few cafés in North Pahlavi Avenue. We have to go that way."

Harriet enjoyed her outing with Keane but with certain reservations for she knew that he was taking the Austrian nurse, Ailsa out that evening. He had mentioned earlier that a patient who had been in hospital for a minor operation had asked them to have dinner at his home. The knowledge was a little unsettling and prevented her from relaxing and taking his friendship for granted. It was illogical, she knew to be at all concerned for she had asserted vehemently that she had no intention of becoming interested in any man.

However the thought kept cropping up in her mind as she drank tea with him and she felt annoyed with herself for allowing it to disturb her. He was a good-looking man with strong, regular features and a very firm jaw. It was no wonder that women were attracted to him.

It would not be wise for me to indulge

in fanciful flights of imagination, she thought as she cast a swift glance at his handsome profile. I'm going to hold on to my independence. He's obviously attracted to Ailsa. If there was no one else I might think differently. But I can't afford to allow myself to get hurt again. It's a pity because I do like him and with any encouragement I might in different circumstances forget my resolution.

"You've been silent a long time," Keane remarked eyeing her curiously. "Have I tired you out or are you bored?"

"Neither. I've been too busy eating." She smiled. "These pastries are delicious. You've only had one. Why is that?"

He grinned. "I have to eat out tonight. I don't want to offend my hostess by refusing her food."

"I had forgotten," she said feigning indifference.

"I might have made some excuse but as Ailsa was invited I had to accept. I didn't want to disappoint her."

"I believe she nursed Mr Payvar after his operation," Harriet said evenly.

"Yes. She became friendly with his family when they came to visit him. She's a charming girl so easy to converse with." With an attempt to appear unconcerned, Harriet said lightly, "You haven't been in the country long and already you have a social life. You evidently find it easy to get on with people. It's a great asset especially in a foreign country."

He frowned. "You make it sound as if it's necessary for me to be popular. It's nothing to do with my personality. A grateful patient wants to show his appreciation. What's wrong with that?"

"I wasn't criticizing."

"It was in your voice." He gazed at her through narrowed eyelids. "I thought we were getting on too well. You don't like me much, do you?"

"Do I really have to answer that?" she asked not at all sure what she ought to say.

"No. I know how you feel. When

someone keeps giving you the cold shoulder it's usual to turn to someone who welcomes your company."

"Is that a dig at me?"

"If you care to take it that way."

She smiled. "I shall be diplomatic and ignore it. It's a pity to spoil an enjoyable afternoon. Now I really ought to go back. And you have a dinner date to get ready for."

The brief ruffling of the surface was over. Keane looked calm and a little remote, Harriet unconcerned. Both of them knew that the truce would not last. Neither wanted to encourage further hostilities.

It was pleasant strolling along the boulevards in the late evening sunshine. The sky had retained that special, porcelain blue colour which was typical of Tehran and the buildings and vegetation were finely outlined against the clear expanse of the heavens.

Harriet sighed with satisfaction. "It's been a beautiful day," she explained as she glanced up at Keane who was walking beside her. "When I first arrived in Tehran I was disappointed. I had expected the city to look more oriental. The traffic and the modern buildings made it seem like any other city."

"It pleases you now?"

"Yes, now I know it's different. Every now and then I have brief glimpses of the Orient. They are more like mirages. Suddenly they are there and I am transported back into the past. Then I discover it's unreal and I'm staring at a picturesque market or an elaborately carved gateway leading into a scented garden."

Keane nodded his head. "I have had similar sensations. Sometimes there is magic in the air. It's difficult to describe and I've not mentioned it to anyone else. It's a relief to hear that you have felt it."

Harriet chuckled. "Perhaps it's just a lively imagination."

"A little maybe, but it's more than that," Keane told her seriously. "I believe it's the air and the city's environment. The Elzburg mountains have a hand in it for they protect the city from the high winds."

"Apparently it becomes unbearably hot in the summer. I wonder how we shall endure it."

"The hospital is air-conditioned. It ought not to affect us."

"At one time the inhabitants used to sleep on their roof tops. It will make a change to go to parties held in the open air. Adina told me that they use a tribal tent lit by candles to eat refreshments in and they dance on a carpet stretched across the lawns."

"A few minutes ago you were accusing me of fraternizing," Keane said in an amused voice. "From the sound of it you intend to do the same."

Harriet smiled. "I know very few people. I have been out quite a lot by myself. North of the city are rich, green valleys where tamarisk edges the streams. I've even seen tulips and some iris on the mountain slopes."

"It's a pity we missed the skiing."

"That is finished by Easter. Stan enjoys it when he can spare the time. I'm planning to visit the Summer Palaces at Shimran. It's only six miles north of the city."

"How long are you intending to stay in Tehran?"

"A year. By then I ought to have seen a few of the superb sights. Adina says one of the beauty spots is in the Lar Valley at the foot of snow-capped Deamavend."

"You seem to have learned a good deal already," Keane commented.

They were approaching the hospital and the fine sun-wrinkles at the corners of Keane's eyes deepened as he gazed at a young man loitering near the gates. He frowned and glanced at Harriet but she was looking with interest across the avenue at a group of bearded Arabs dressed in colourful, flowing robes and white turbans. Lithe and fine-featured she guessed that they had come from Arabia for by now she was beginning to distinguish the different races.

Keane asked abruptly, "Isn't that the man I saw you talking to a couple of weeks ago?"

Harriet turned a startled glance at the road ahead. After the well-groomed appearance of the Arabs the young man's shabby clothes was a shocking contrast.

"It's Yousaf!" she exclaimed. "I wonder what he is doing here?"

"Waiting for you, I imagine," Keane sounded disapproving. "Shall I tell him to clear off?"

"No!" Harriet looked distressed. "He is shy of Westerners so would you mind walking on? I will have a word with him and catch you up."

Keane did not look too pleased at her suggestion but did not argue. Harriet waited until he was out of earshot and then went across to Yousaf.

"Hello! How is Nafisa and the baby?" she asked regarding him with undisguised curiosity.

Yousaf smiled sheepishly. "They are well." He spoke hesitantly for he did not speak English as fluently as his wife. "Nafisa asked me to come. We have a man with us who says he knows you. He has written this."

Looking puzzled Harriet took the folded sheet torn from a notebook and opened it. Then as she read the few scrawled words her face whitened and her body stiffened as if with shock.

"Is he very ill?" she asked in a strained voice.

Yousaf nodded his head gazing at her with mournful, brown eyes. "He wanders in his mind. Nafisa mentioned you and he became very excited and pleaded with her to get in touch with you. We fear for his life if we move on. The elders are growing impatient and want to leave him behind but Nafisa asked them to wait until I had seen you."

"Are you very far from the city?"

"We are in the desert a few miles

beyond Saveh. It is on the old caravan route."

"Are there any roads? Could I get there on my own?"

"I am prepared to take you. I can get donkeys."

Harriet shook her head. "It would take too long. A car would be quicker."

"It can only take you some of the way."

Harriet stared at him helplessly. "Does that mean we would have to go on foot when the road finishes?"

"Perhaps two or three kilometres."

Her face lightened. "That's not too bad." She raised her head and glanced towards the hospital and with something of a shock realized that Keane was still waiting for her. She had forgotten about him.

If it had been Stan Maddox she would have called him over and discussed the problem but she did not want to tell Keane. However she had no option for Keane strode across to her to enquire what was wrong. He had noticed how pale she had become and was worried because she was looking distressed.

"Can I help?" he asked after a swift glance at Harriet and her companion. "Do you feel ill, Harriet? You look as if you have seen a ghost."

She hesitated then pulled him aside. "Someone I used to know has asked for my help," she said in a shaky voice. "Yousaf says he is very ill."

"Where?" Keane asked curtly.

"He's with Yousaf's tribe near Saveh."

Keane turned back to the Iranian. "What is the matter with him? Why didn't you bring him to the hospital?"

Yousaf's brown face became frightened. "He did not want to come," he stuttered.

Harriet swiftly intervened. "It's a rifle wound. He stumbled into their camp exhausted and without food or drink. One of the women extracted the bullet but he's very weak and not improving. Yousaf is frightened that he will die. Then there will be enquiries. They do not want trouble with the authorities."

Keane frowned. "This man is important to you?" he asked gruffly.

Harriet pushed back her hair with nervous fingers then reluctantly answered in an uneven voice, "He was once. He is the man I was engaged to."

His eyes narrowed. "I see . . . It's strange he didn't want to be brought to Tehran. Do you think he might he in the country illegally?"

"It's possible. He could have been shot crossing the frontier." She broke off then after a few seconds said in a distressed voice, "You do understand? I have to get to him. He has asked for me."

"How did he know where you were?"

"Nafisa spoke about me."

"You are planning to go on your own?"

"Yousaf will take me by donkey, he says, but I shall hire a car."

"You can't go alone. It would be very foolish. I can borrow a Landrover. We shall need food, drink, sleeping bags as well as medical equipment."

She looked startled. "We? You are coming with me?"

"Naturally. You don't think I'm going to allow you to wander off into the desert with this Nomad, do you?"

A glimmer of amusement showed in her eyes. "It's good of you but I can't expect you to become involved in my problems."

"I'm already involved," he said gruffly. "Luckily I have a few days' leave due. What about you?"

"I can have a week if it can be arranged."

"That's no problem. I will see to it. Do cheer up! Nothing is as bad as it seems."

She released a deep sigh of relief. "It was the suddenness of it. I haven't heard from Morris for over a year and now this. Having you with me would relieve my mind. Morris may be very seriously ill."

Keane said briskly, "Tell your friend

that we will meet him at six o'clock tomorrow morning, right here."

Yousaf looked pleased when she explained. He smiled and nodded his head. "I will be here," he said simply before he moved off.

Keane and Harriet walked through the open gates and took the main drive to the hospital. Harriet was looking dazed and worried. Her spirits had touched zero when she had read that note from Morris. It had been so unexpected. She had known that he had taken an engineering post in the Middle East but that covered a vast area. He could have been anywhere in Saudi Arabia.

"The news has upset you," Keane said regarding her with watchful grey eyes. "You still care for this man?"

She thought she could detect criticism in his deep voice and her mouth compressed with irritation. "It's not easy to forget," she said defensively. "I thought it was finished. It was all over months ago."

"Now it's worrying you again." Keane's face darkened and he relapsed into silence. When he resumed talking it was in a more kindly tone of voice. "There's no need for you to go. Yousaf can direct me to the camp."

Harriet shook her head. "I appreciate your offer but I shall have to go. Morris says he is in trouble. He has asked me to help him. It's not your problem."

He smiled tolerantly. "Very well if you are determined to be made uncomfortable. If you become upset when you receive a note from him how are you going to react when you see him?"

Perturbed and distressed she said sharply, "I don't know. I can't tell you that." Aware of the keen scrutiny of his smoke-grey eyes she quickened her pace and arrived at the main entrance slightly out of breath.

Keane glanced quickly at his wrist-watch. "I will arrange for our leave of absence before I go out this evening," he said briskly. "We can meet tomorrow morning just before six o'clock. Out here if you wish."

"Will you have time to get supplies?"

"A phone call will ensure we have the Landrover and any supplies we might need. I have a friend who works at the Embassy. There's no problem there." He smiled. "Knowing people does have its advantages. The medical supplies you can leave to me."

"What will you say to Sister in Charge of the hospital?"

"The truth." Noticing how alarmed she had become he went on smoothly, "She needn't be told of the personal angle. I can be diplomatic if I have to."

"Thank you. You will have to forgive me if I seem over anxious."

His eyes softened. "You have had a shock. You are frightened. There's no need to be. Try to consider it as all in the day's work. A man is injured. You are going to nurse him."

She nodded. "Yes. That is the

sensible way to consider it. I feel better now."

"Good. I will see you tomorrow then. Don't bring too much luggage. I know what you women are. A couple of days and you imagine you need your entire wardrobe."

Harriet smiled to herself as she walked across the entrance hall and took the lift up to her room. Keane had been very kind, surprisingly so. Her agitation had left her and she felt calm and vaguely detached as if it were all happening to someone else.

This happy state remained with her for most of the evening but when she went to bed early she was unable to sleep for a long time. Innumerable difficulties presented themselves and she worried over them continually. Supposing Morris was in trouble with the police? Taking Keane along might prove awkward. He would be bound to insist on reporting the accident to them. I ought not to have told him, she thought worriedly. I could have nursed Morris and found out what the position is. He's not going to thank me for taking Keane into my confidence. Yet if Morris is desperately ill I shall need Keane. And Morris' life is the most important thing. I might not be able to save him. Yes, it is best that Keane go with me. Anyway I may be worrying unnecessarily.

Lulled into a sense of security she eventually fell into a deep sleep just after midnight. The alarm clock woke her at five fifteen and she sprang out of bed at once, wide awake and acutely conscious of the importance of the task which lay ahead. As she slipped into her dressing-gown she heard the swelling notes of the bells from a camel-train and immediately her thoughts flew to Morris who was somewhere out there in the desert.

She took a quick shower and dressed in blue jeans and a white blouse leaving her dark blue jacket on the bed ready for when she left. She made tea and drank it then added last minute items to her hold-all as she munched a few biscuits. They might not stop for a meal until much later and she did not want to make a nuisance of herself by feeling faint.

As she did not have many clothes with her it had not been difficult to choose which she would take. A pair of slacks and two or three blouses would suffice. Usually she pinned her hair up under her cap but today she left it loose. It would be cooler and easier to keep tidy that way.

She wrote a quick note to Adina explaining that she was taking a few days' leave and would see her when she returned, put it in an addressed envelope and left it on the dressing-table. One of the maids would deliver it after they had cleaned the room.

'That's everything, I think,' she murmured as she cast a quick last look at the room. 'I haven't heard from Keane so presumably he was able to arrange my leave.'

She did not encounter anyone as

she went along the corridor and took the lift down to the ground floor. This pleased her for she did not feel in the mood for explanations. Keane was waiting outside the Staff entrance looking as well-groomed in his leisure clothes as he did when walking the wards.

Glancing at his sheep-skin jacket she said curiously, "Won't you be too warm in that?"

He grinned. "I was advised to take it. Apparently it can get cold in the desert at night." He lifted his right foot and showed her a rope-soled shoe. "I was given these too."

She smiled. "Your friend is thorough. He evidently thinks you will be doing some hiking."

"It's as well to be prepared," he said lightly as he took her hold-all from her and led the way to a Landrover which was parked a short distance away.

"Good gracious!" Harriet exclaimed when she saw the contents of the van.

"You have enough supplies there for an army."

"We are to act as a minor Health Corps and give supplies to those in need. The surplus has to be returned."

Harriet laughed. "It's to be a busman's vacation then!"

"One favour deserves another. I had to stress the advantages of nurse and doctor roaming in the desert wastes."

Harriet chuckled. The fear and gloom of the previous evening had disappeared. Keane was presenting it as a glorious adventure. She was grateful for the way he was taking it. He could have been overbearing and disagreeable making her aware that he was doing her a favour. But from the way he was acting he was giving the impression that he was enjoying the novelty.

Yousaf was waiting outside the hospital gates and Harriet noticed that his brown eyes were alight with excitement and guessed that it was because he was going to travel by car. It would he a change for him after mules and donkeys.

In spite of the early hour there was considerable traffic in the centre of the city. Keane was fairly used to driving about the capital which was fortunate for the carelessness of the drivers could bring on a heart attack. Cars stopped suddenly to allow passengers to alight giving no signals regardless of the vehicles behind and it was quite usual for taxis to make U turns in the middle of the road. Damaged cars littered the roads and movable signs could bewilder drivers unaccustomed to them.

Keane took the road south out of the city and when he was reaching the outskirts asked, "Where do we make for now?"

Harriet turned to glance at Yousaf who was sitting in the back. "Do you know the quickest route, Yousaf?" she asked.

He nodded. "Go to Ray then Kahrizak on the Qum road. I will tell you when to turn off."

"The roads are good in spite of it being desert," Keane remarked after they left Kahrizak. "I've noticed one or two gas stations."

Harriet said, "I see you have a full tank. I hope it will be enough to get us there and back to the main road."

"I have another can in the back. Do you know anything about Saveh?" Keane enquired. The asphalt road was in good repair and as the traffic had thinned out he could relax a little.

"Adina mentioned it a few weeks ago. It's situated on a not very fertile desert plain. The road to it is far from towns and little used. Saveh was built where the Hamadan Road crosses the old caravan route. There is a track to Kazvin which passes the ruined caravanserais of Dung and Jib."

"We won't have to go that far, I hope."

"I don't think so. Yousaf says his tribe are camped just beyond Saveh. It's supposed to be the site where the Three Wise Men came from with gold, frankincense and myrrh. And Marco Polo stayed there on his travels. It's just a derelict town now with two ancient mosques."

Yousaf interrupted her to exclaim, "We come to camel track soon. It will be quicker than on this road."

Keane slowed down and turned right on to a lane worn smooth by camels and trucks. They were soon deep in a region of desert with dried up river beds and after several halts to extricate them from sand because the track was no longer firm, Keane was doubting the wisdom of following Yousaf's directions. Adding to the discomfort the sky had become overcast and a strong wind had sprung up.

"It doesn't look too promising," Keane muttered. "I hope we're not in for a sand storm."

"It might be a good idea to stop soon," Harriet said. "There's an old wall over there. It would shelter us from the wind and sand. We ought to have something to eat."

"Good idea." Keane brought the Landrover to a halt and climbed out stiffly.

Harriet was thankful to be able to stretch her limbs but she was surprised at the force of the wind. She left the Landrover with alacrity when Keane told her to go ahead and ploughed through the sand to the walls of the old ruined fort. When Keane and Yousaf came over with cardboard boxes of food and drink Harriet began to unpack them. She found that the contents had been chosen with care. There were rolls, hard boiled eggs, meat patties, breast of chicken rolled and stuffed, tinned rice and kebabs on skewers plus yoghourt, cans of beer, bottled orange juice and bags of nuts.

"Your friend didn't intend us to starve!" she exclaimed. "I hope he remembered a can opener."

"I did," Keane grinned as he pulled one from his trouser pocket. "I've been caught out before so I made a point of bringing one. Eat as much as you want.

There's more in the Landrover."

Yousaf was shy and sat apart from Keane and Harriet until they told him to join them. Harriet found plastic plates and cups in one of the boxes and as Keane opened the tins she prepared the food arranging it on top of two of the boxes.

They were too hungry to complain about the grains of sand which had found its way into the food and drink. That was a minor detail.

"I haven't enjoyed a meal so much for ages," Harriet exclaimed when they had finished. "How am I going to clean the plates? We shall need them again."

Keane grinned. "Have you forgotten your camping lore? We used to use earth."

"Of course! Sand will clean them." But when Harriet had rubbed sand over them she said doubtfully, "I suppose it's too much to expect to find water. If this was a fort surely there's a water hole?"

"There is some at the back of the ruins," Yousaf said. "Come, I will show you."

Keane and Harriet followed him but had to smile when they saw the tiny trickle of brown water oozing from the old water-hole. But it was enough to rinse the plates and cups and Harriet felt well pleased.

"I filled a couple of cans with water before we left," Keane told her. "You could have had some of that."

"We ought to conserve that for the engine. I noticed it was steaming before we stopped."

"It's this road. It might be all right for camels but totally unsuitable for motorized vehicles. It's nearly one o'clock. We made good time until we turned off into the desert. I think we ought to push on. We are bound to get stuck every now and then."

The wind dropped and the sun revealed itself sending powerful rays on to the unprotected desolate land. After half an hour it was like an oven inside the vehicle. The engine was labouring and Keane stopped to give it time to cool down.

A band of Nomads passed with the men and women walking beside their donkeys laden with tents, carpets and bouncing children. The women were dressed in long, colourful skirts made of patchwork and the men, some of whom carried rifles, had jackets made from skins. Their faces were brown and lined, their hair hidden by swathes of fine material which could be pulled up over their mouths. They darted curious glances at the Landrover as they went by and the children shouted and waved.

"Do you know them?" Harriet asked Yousaf after they had climbed back into the vehicle and started off once more.

"No. They are Kurds. We are from Luristan."

Still the heat from the sun beat down on them relentlessly. The desert stretched around them rolling like a vast and monotonous sea devouring the heat. Before them a faint haze wavered and beckoned.

"I wish I had brought a bikini with me," Harriet said flippantly. "Clothes seem ridiculous."

Keane grinned. "Take them off if it makes you feel cooler."

"You will shock Yousaf," she replied quickly her face even pinker than it had been before.

"Seriously though, clothes prevent the sun from getting to you," Keane told her. "So long as they are loose and comfortable."

Harriet glanced at Yousaf who was smiling. "Why don't you dress as the Arabs do?"

"Sometimes we do but the robes are expensive. The women make most of our clothes from scraps."

Harriet wished that she had not asked and was relieved that Yousaf seemed unconcerned. She supposed that it was because he was so used to being poor. Yet he appeared content.

Envy apparently was non-existent. If it had been he would not be so happy. We Westerners are spoilt, she thought feeling ashamed. We take so much for granted.

She heard Keane mutter an oath, felt the Landrover shudder violently and was thrown forward on to the windscreen. Fear gripped her by the throat. Her head was spinning and she could not see. Then a vast blackness encompassed her and she slumped down into the seat.

Fear showed for a second in Keane's grey eyes when he noticed her face drained of colour. Then moving swiftly he opened the door and climbed out. Within a few minutes he had Harriet outstretched on a rug at the side of the Landrover.

Seeing that Yousaf was hovering looking distressed he said curtly, "Get one of the cans of water."

Harriet opened her eyes to find Keane leaning over her gently bathing her face. There seemed to be a great deal of water pouring over her and she protested feebly.

"You're drowning me! What happened?" She made a movement to sit up and exclaimed, "Oh, my head!"

"Keep still!" he commanded. "You've given me enough frights for one afternoon."

She felt the needle prick her arm and protested again but almost soundlessly. Alarmed she gazed into his amused face.

"It's only a pain-killer. How do you feel now?"

"Fine," she lied.

"You struck your head and passed out. There doesn't appear to be other damage. But you will have to be quiet for awhile. Yousaf and I are going to push the Landrover out. We struck loose sand and a gap in the track."

"I shall be in the way here," she said glancing up at the side of the vehicle.

"I'm going to put you back in the car. When I bend down put your arms around my neck."

103

She had not noticed before how dark his eyebrows were. As he lifted her his rough cheek touched her face and she caught a near glance of his thickly fringed grey eyes. Every nerve in her body was aware of him as he held her close. Then she was back in her seat with Keane smiling at her sardonically.

"Mind you stay there. No hopping out to help!"

I couldn't even if I wanted to she thought still in a state of bemusement. Too much is happening too fast. Keane held me as tenderly as a child. The blow on my head has made me foolish. He's got too much to contend with. I really must pull myself together. Perhaps it's the sun and I'm light-headed. I could have sworn he was going to kiss me. But he wouldn't with Yousaf looking on. I'm imagining it. It's not happening. She put a hand to her clammy temples. Oh yes, it is, she told herself sharply. Whatever made him pour so much water over me. I'm soaked to the skin!

By the time Keane and Yousaf had dug the vehicle out Harriet had recovered her usual calm slant on things. This was fortunate for when Keane slid into the driving seat he was hot and irritable.

"Have a drink before you go on," Harriet advised him.

"It will only make me hotter." His eyes glinted. "Evidently you have recovered. Getting bossy again."

She relapsed into a hurt silence resolving not to speak to him again until he was in a better frame of mind. They passed the remnants of a camp close to a water-hole then drove slowly farther into an arid grassless expanse.

Yousaf said suddenly. "There is no need to go through Saveh. Soon you will notice another track on your left. If you think it is wide enough it will lead you to our camp."

Keane frowned. "Is it as bad as this one?"

"It is not so good but it will save time."

"It won't if we get stuck," Keane said sourly.

"Then we will walk. The men will come for your supplies with donkeys."

"Very well," Keane replied reluctantly. "At the rate we are going we won't be there until nightfall." He turned his head and smiled faintly at Harriet. "How's the head?" he asked.

"Not too bad. I shall feel better when we are out of this vehicle."

"I hope you are right. Yousaf's idea of a short walk may not agree with ours. You couldn't take a long stretch on your feet now."

"Don't worry about me," she said.

He lifted a dark eyebrow. "That's easier said than done. However it can't be much farther now. We are near Saveh."

Keane drove as far as it was possible to do so. The route had not been used lately and was thick with loose sand which made it barely discernible.

"That's it then," Keane said curtly as the vehicle came to a halt with its wheels churning the loose sand. "We shall have to use Shank's pony from here."

4

KEANE packed some medical supplies in his own case, put Harriet's hold-all on the sand beside it, then locked the doors of the Landrover. Then he looked at Harriet to see if she was all right.

"We can leave you here and come back for you with one of Yousaf's donkeys," he said.

"Certainly not!" she said indignantly. "A walk will do me good."

Keane grinned. "You're an optimist. Let's start then. Yousaf can carry your hold-all."

The only one of them who seemed happy at the thought of trudging across soft sand was Yousaf. But then he was well used to it for the Nomads usually travelled on foot leaving the donkeys to carry their tents and belongings and sometimes the sick. Keane and Harriet soon tired and lagged behind leaving Yousaf who continually hummed to himself, forging ahead.

"This isn't like the deserts of Arabia," Keane remarked rather breathlessly. "It's neither one thing nor the other. It's part desert, part plain yet semi-fertile. Pity we couldn't have come on horseback."

Harriet chuckled. "We have too many supplies. I hope we can get a wash when we arrive."

"I doubt that." Keane grinned. "You've become too civilized. But if you're good I might spare a drop from one of the cans."

Harriet laughed. "I can't misbehave here. It's a deal!"

"You will have to wait until the donkeys arrive with it. At the rate we are going that might be tomorrow morning."

"You are pessimistic!"

An hour passed and Keane began to cast anxious glances at Harriet who was beginning to stumble frequently.

He would have called a halt but Yousaf was too far ahead and he did not want to lose sight of him.

"Take my arm," he urged when Harriet fell to her knees. "I knew this would be too much for you."

"My shoes keep slipping," she said defensively, obstinately refusing to admit she was beaten.

However she was sensible enough to lean on his arm and after that she did not fall. Yousaf had disappeared from sight when shrill childish voices warned them that they were approaching the camp. Then they were over a ridge and looking down on the flat roofs of half a dozen black tents. They were large and high enough to walk about in as they soon discovered.

Harriet's first thought was to find Morris but Keane urged her to wait. Nafisa came from one of the tents and ran towards them. She greeted them warmly kissing Harriet's hands and telling her to go in and rest.

Harriet hesitated then because the

brown-faced men were crowding around them she followed Nafisa into the tent. The ground was covered with carpet and two women were reclining on it with their elbows on cushions.

"Where is the wounded man?" Harriet asked. "We ought to see him first."

"That's why I brought you in here. He's over there behind that curtain," Nafisa said.

Keane brushed by them and went across to the man lying on a bed of skins. Morris was so still that Harriet caught her breath in alarm.

"Is he alive?" she asked fearfully. "His skin is so pallid."

Keane examined Morris swiftly feeling his pulse and lifting his eyelids. "He's unconscious," he said curtly then turned to Nafisa and asked quietly, "How long has he been like this?"

"Off and on ever since he came to us. But since yesterday morning he hasn't spoken sensibly. I went to give him something to eat and found him like this. Desma, she is an old woman who understands these things, took the bullet from his shoulder the day he came. But he has not responded to her treatment and we feared for his life. That is why I sent Yousaf to you."

"That was very sensible of you." Keane smiled at her kindly, "I shall have to clean up. Could you bring me a bowl and hot water?"

Morris opened his eyes and stared at them. There was no recognition in the wild feverish glance. Keane spoke to him soothingly pushing him back gently on to the bed of skins. Then he opened his case and took out his box of instruments and medical equipment.

Harriet gazed at the man who once had meant so much to her with distress in her blue eyes. "Are we going to be able to save him?" she asked, her voice shaking with emotion. "There's nothing of him! He was such a strong vigorous man. Now he's practically a skeleton."

"Fever can do that. I've seen men

ravaged before. Pull yourself together, Harriet! I know it's painful for you but this isn't the time to indulge yourself."

"Yes, you are right," she said contritely. "It was a shock seeing him so ill."

"I understand. Ah, here's Nafisa! Hold the bowl for me so I can scrub up. There's soap in my case."

Keane immersed his hands and arms in the hot water and soaped them thoroughly, then asked Harriet to pour some surgical spirit over them. Harriet cleaned her hands also before she assisted Keane who had begun to remove the grubby dressing covering the wound. She gasped when the damage was revealed.

"No wonder he's feverish!" she exclaimed. "It's gangrenous."

Keane said grimly, "Clean it up as best you can and put a clean dressing on it. I will prepare a shot of penicillin. After that you can give him a good wash or if you don't feel up to it, I will. I bet he's not been clean since he came. You can tell Nafisa that we will replace the water when we have our cans."

"I will see to him," Harriet said calmly. "Hot water will do wonders."

"Pity we don't know if he's allergic to penicillin," Keane said.

"If he is then he won't improve and we will know." Harriet smiled faintly. "We can only do what we think is best."

"Relax, Harriet. There's no cause for alarm. I can't do any more for the moment. I will see if Yousaf has arranged to have some of the supplies brought in."

It was nightfall before Harriet had finished seeing to Morris. The women had lit lamps so that she could see what she was doing and one of them had come over to help. But Harriet shook her head and the woman looking vaguely surprised had gone away. When Nafisa looked in Harriet explained why she had refused to allow the woman to help her.

"I think I have offended her," she said. "Would you apologize for me, Nafisa? I think you understand how careful we have to be."

Nafisa nodded her head and smiled. "I ought to. I discovered that soap and water is almost your religion. It is difficult for them. When they are in the desert they cannot wash. But I will make it clear to her."

Harriet went outside to breathe in the cooler air. It had been stifling inside the tent. Keane joined her after a few minutes and they strolled together a few yards away from the camp. There was no moon but the stars, huge and bright were so brilliant in the dark, velvety sky that they formed shadows on the dunes. The wind had dropped and the air was refreshingly cool. Harriet caught whiffs of smoke from the fire the Nomads had lit. A woman was cooking something in a black pot and two others were holding kebabs over the smoke.

"I wonder what they are cooking," Harriet said idly.

"Stew, probably goat," Keane replied. "We shall have to get your young man out of here, tomorrow. He ought to be in hospital."

Harriet frowned. "That might be awkward for him if he did come into the country illegally."

"He doesn't appear to have any papers so we can't examine his passport. We can't leave him here."

"No, I realize that."

"Don't look so worried. Our immediate worry is his life. Anything else must take second place. You do agree with me?"

He stopped, turned to her and took her hands. Her face looked pale and delicate in the light from the stars, her eyes hauntingly dark and unhappy.

"Don't look so unhappy, my dear," he said gruffly. "You cut me in two. If only I could help."

"You are helping just by being here,"

she said smiling at him gratefully. She saw the tenderness in his eyes and nearly disgraced herself by bursting into tears. The longing to fling herself into his arms to be held safe and secure against his hard chest was almost too much. She swallowed the lump in her throat, blinked back the stinging tears and pulled her hands from his grasp. "It was very good of you to come," she said unevenly.

"I wanted to. There's no need to thank me. We will see how he is tomorrow. There's no need to make any decision right now." Keane smiled wryly. "I suppose I shall have to sleep in one of the tents with the men. If I was positive I might not be needed I would walk back to the Landrover and sleep there."

Harriet said, "I shall sit up with Morris."

"Do you feel hungry? Yousaf has had some supplies brought in."

Harriet smiled. "I thought you were anticipating the stew."

"Somehow I don't fancy that. Of course if we hadn't anything else and we were really hungry it might taste like manna from heaven."

"I don't feel hungry either. We can have a big breakfast. I hope we can share our food with the Nomads."

"That was my intention. We have to show our appreciation. It was good of them to take your friend in and care for him. I believe the women of these tribes are well used to extracting bullets."

"Their own men are tough enough to survive. Living the way they do needs terrific powers of endurance. I feel sorry for the women."

"They look contented enough."

"That's because they know no other way of life. Nafisa has acquired some knowledge of how other women live. I ought to have asked after her baby."

"You can do that tomorrow. I think we ought to go back and take another look at our patient."

It seemed a long night for both of them. Harriet dozed off occasionally but was awakened by the slightest movement of her patient. He was very restless and breathing heavily with occasional mutterings which were incoherent. The tent was half-filled with women and children and the air was oppressive. Harriet wondered how Keane was faring and guessed that he would not be able to endure the lack of fresh air in the tent for the entire night.

When she saw him the next morning she was heavy-eyed and weary and expected him to be the same but he appeared bright and cheerful. "You evidently slept well," she said languidly.

"It wasn't too bad. After an hour inside I took my sleeping bag outside and slept on the sand."

Harriet chuckled. "I guessed you would. I couldn't go through another night like that."

"You don't look too good. How's your patient? Did he give you any trouble?"

"No, although he was very restless.

He was sleeping when I left him so I think the penicillin is having an effect."

"I will give him another jab if it's safe for me to enter the tent. I vote we move him out then and have our breakfast in the Landrover."

"You don't seem to be enjoying your stay with the Nomads," she teased.

He grinned. "There's no point in prolonging the agony. Anyway these people want to move on. They will be delighted to see the back of us. We can't wait here until Morris recovers consciousness. It might take days."

"Yes. We can't do anything else. I will go and tell Nafisa what we intend to do."

Yousaf was very helpful. With the aid of two other young men he improvised a stretcher with two poles and skins so that Morris could be carried easily. Harriet nodded her approval when she saw it.

"That's fine," she said. "It can also be used to carry more supplies back to your camp. You can have all we won't need."

Yousaf's eyes brightened. "Some of the canned beer as well?"

"Why not," Harriet said smilingly and the young men laughed.

She turned to Nafisa who had emerged from a tent carrying her baby son. "Thanks for caring for the wounded man. There will be some powdered milk with the supplies we are going to leave behind. You know how to use it, don't you?"

"Yes. Are you going so soon?" Nafisa exclaimed looking disappointed.

"The injured man ought to be in hospital. Will you thank your people. They have been very kind."

The girl shrugged her shoulders. "We would always help those in need whatever their race. If he had recovered quickly it would not have mattered. But the elders want to move farther south into the desert. We could not take him with us. They have become impatient at the delay. However I think they have

121

been well rewarded. There is no need to thank them."

"Your baby looks healthy. He's put on weight quickly. Now I've seen how you live I realize how difficult it is for you to keep him clean."

Nafisa nodded. "If I had not been in the hospital I would not have noticed. Now it worries me that I cannot care for him properly."

Harriet smiled sympathetically. "I wouldn't be too disturbed. You were brought up in the desert and most children survive. I believe you are sensible enough to come to terms with your old ways of life and use the knowledge you have gained to improve conditions."

Harriet left her to go back to Morris. Keane was in the tent examining the wounded man. He was frowning and did not look too pleased.

"Is he worse?" Harriet asked anxiously.

"He's in a critical state. It's these conditions. They are impossible. We have to get him out."

"Yes, I agree. Yousaf has made a stretcher. We can take him right away. I will ask to have it brought in here."

The Nomad women looked on curiously as Morris was transferred to the stretcher and carried outside. Harriet and Keane followed carrying their cases and saw that the stretcher bearers were already climbing the ridge out of camp.

"*Khoda hafez! Salam aleykoum!*" The men and women chanted and Nafisa called out in English, "Goodbye! May peace be with you!"

The Landrover had become covered with sand during the night and they had to get rid of that before they could open the doors. Then Harriet and Keane took out the supplies they had promised to give the Nomads leaving a few for themselves. It was easy after that to carry Morris inside and make him comfortable on sacks and blankets. Yousaf and his friends picked up the loaded stretcher after they had thanked them and said "goodbye" and were soon walking rapidly away.

"I hope they feel happy about their supplies," Keane remarked as he climbed in and started the engine.

Harriet chuckled. "The young men would have been content with a few cans of beer. I don't think they expected anything. They are used to helping people lost in the desert. They are hospitable people."

"It beats me how they survive. They never have any money, everything is gained by barter and that can't be very profitable for they have little to bargain with."

"It's the way of life they prefer," Harriet pointed out after they had started off. "They rear some cattle. I expect that's why they want to move south. Once they have crossed the desert the land becomes more fertile in the valleys beneath the Zagros mountains."

"That's a devilish way to go. I wouldn't care for their life."

"You're not conditioned to it. They

are freer than most people."

"But what a price to pay! Anyway I'm pleased we were able to give them a few things."

Harriet said thoughtfully, "I wonder if they have a tin-opener?"

Keane laughed. "You would think of that! If they haven't they will soon find a way to open the cans."

"After I met Nafisa I began to ask questions about her tribe. Adina told me that they are noted for stealing and will rob anyone they come across."

"You think they robbed your young man?"

"No, I don't," she said sharply. "I do wish you would stop referring to him as my young man!"

Keane flicked a shrewd glance at her. "There must be some truth in it otherwise you wouldn't be so touchy."

"It was over months ago," she said flatly then went on as if it was of no importance. "Adina also told me that the Lurs were rulers once of a vast area and were known as the Atabegs.

Their dynasty was wiped out by one of the Shahs who killed their rulers. So now they are rebels, hating any government or laws. I suspect they helped Morris because he is in trouble with the law."

"You could be right. They would be helpless without their women-folk. Did you notice that they were doing most of the work?"

Harriet chuckled. "That's not uncommon in our part of the world! I was aware of how much they do. They milk the goats, weave carpets, make tents and saddle bags, cook and feed the men, children and animals."

Keane grinned. "You haven't left much for the men to do."

"They give the orders." She laughed. "To be fair they do grow a few crops when they settle long enough and they travel miles to the towns to sell their cattle and barter for food. They have to be just as tough as the women."

Harriet opened her cosmetic bag

which she had used for her soap, flannel and other odds and ends and took out a bottle of eau de cologne. She was bathing the injured man's forehead and face with it when Keane exclaimed irritably and pulled the vehicle up with a jolt.

"Confound it! I think we've got a puncture."

He was right as they soon discovered when they climbed down. Not one but two punctures!

"One is bad enough!" Keane exclaimed. "I bet there's only one spare wheel."

"No, there's two," Harriet told him. "I remember seeing it when we made room for Morris. We might as well have our breakfasts before we start."

"I don't like leaving Morris inside. It's too hot."

Harriet glanced at the barren wastes of sand about them. "There's no shade at all. He will have to stay where he is. I will prepare something to eat and drink. Then we can munch as we go.

We won't have to stay here too long then."

When she had finished she gave Keane all the assistance she could handing him the various tools he requested. "It's rather like being in Theatre," she said laughingly.

Keane smiled wryly and wiped his forehead with greasy fingers. "I trust it's cleaner there and not quite so warm. Take a look at the patient. I've nearly finished."

Harriet wet the injured man's lips with orange juice then bathed his face and hands with her eau de cologne. He was still unconscious but his pulse rate had improved. His colour also looked more natural.

"He seems better," she said. "You've been quick. Your friend at the Embassy was wise to give us two extra wheels."

Keane who was rubbing his face with a towel muttered, "He's used to motoring in Iran. Parts of that road we came on dropped a foot deep. No wonder we had blow-outs!"

Harriet tactfully handed him one of the opened cans of beer which he drank thirstily. But he refused anything to eat. When he climbed back into the driving seat he was not in a very good mood. He was hot, tired and annoyed at the delay. He was also irritated by Harriet's concern for Morris. It was petty and unjust and being aware of the fact only made him more edgy. It was the sight of her deft fingers gently stroking Morris' sandy hair from his forehead which finally got under his skin.

"There's no point in doing that!" he exclaimed roughly. "He's not aware of anything."

She looked at him in surprise. "He's feverish. I'm trying to keep him as cool as possible."

"Fan him. Here you can use my hat," he said curtly.

Harriet waited until they reached a smooth patch of sand and were progressing fairly fast before she spoke again. Keane seemed more relaxed now that they were under way.

"I believe the best way to drive across sand is very fast," she said.

"That's correct but dangerous if you run into soft sand or underground drops. I'm taking it steady. I don't want to knock you unconscious again. I notice the bruise has come out. Is it painful?"

"No. I had forgotten about it."

"I'm sorry I was so irritable just now. I was impatient at the delay. This darn engine isn't behaving itself. Sand in it I reckon."

"It's become very windy. I hope we're not running into a sand storm."

Half an hour later Keane was forced to stop. He had been going very slowly, finally just slithering and crawling along. The wind was whipping up the sand and he was driving blind.

"It's useless!" he ejaculated. "We shall have to wait until it's over."

"At least it's cooler," Harriet said. "Do you want a drink?"

"Good idea. I will have something to eat as well."

130

Harriet handed him a tuna fish sandwich and a plastic cup filled with orange juice. "I'm sorry there's no more canned beer."

"I don't like it all that much." He munched hungrily, drank the orange juice then exclaimed, "The wind is dropping! It wasn't very severe after all. We can go on now."

He climbed out closing the door swiftly behind him. Even so a blast of sand caught Harriet in the face and she had to fumble for the towel to wipe her face. When she could see clearly again she noticed that Keane was sweeping the sand from the wind-screen. She had the towel ready for him when he climbed in gasping for breath.

At first the Landrover refused to budge but after several attempts Keane finally got it moving although now that the track was covered over with loose sand it was difficult to keep on course. Then just as they had settled down to a steady speed the vehicle dived suddenly into a bank of loose sand and shuddered to a halt. Feeling severely jolted and shocked they clambered out to inspect the damage.

The wind had died down and the sky was as clear as it had been early that morning. Stretching as far as their eyes could see was a barren, waterless terrain with an endless series of sand dunes. Harriet's face was tight with grit, her throat parched, for, it was intensely hot. Her heart sank when she saw that the Landrover was up to the hub-caps in sand.

"How is our patient?" Keane asked.

"He took the jolt better than we did. He seems quieter now."

Keane's face cracked into a stiff smile. "Then cheer up, do! It's not so bad. We shall have to shovel ourselves out. Get the required tool."

Harriet chuckled as she handed him the shovel. "Your friend thought of everything."

"Not quite," Keane said seriously. "We could have done with some sand tracks. They can be stretched in front of the vehicle in tricky spots."

Keane began to shovel the sand away grimly. He was not at all sure that it was going to be the answer but luckily came to firmer sand and was able to form a gradient in front of the vehicle.

"Keep a watchful eye on Morris. It's going to shake a lot," he said after he had climbed in and started the engine.

But they were lucky this time. After vibrating violently the Landrover took the slope like a veteran and they were able to continue in a faster and smoother manner.

"I'm surprised any car can stand up to that kind of punishment," Harriet remarked.

Keane smiled grimly. "I wouldn't care to test its durability too much. If my memory is correct that black line on the horizon to the right is where we stopped on our way to the camp."

Soon the mud walls of the fort became visible and both of them felt considerably happier because they knew they would soon be off the camel track. They came across an occasional stunted tree with scraggy branches and patches of straw-like grass then more ruins and scattered shrubs which even had shades of green in their withered branches. Another mile was covered and then they had left the hazardous camel track with its unsuspected spots of soft sand and dangerous gaps, and were travelling fast on an asphalted road, leaving the wind-beaten desert behind them.

Viewing the yellow stretches of sand either side of them Harriet remarked, "I imagined that all this was desert. Now I know there is a difference. I've seen the real desert."

Keane turned quickly and smiled at her. "I'm afraid you're mistaken. What we've been through is a picnic compared to the desolate wastes in Arabia, North Africa and central Iran. So far we've only skimmed the fringe of the desert."

Harriet laughed. "Another illusion gone! If I had any romantic fancies about it before they have gone now. I can understand why the desert men are merciless and unyielding, insisting on keeping their women hidden and refusing to co-operate with the law. It's a case of survival."

Keane cast a twinkling glance at her. "Some of those Nomads were fine looking men. Didn't your girlish heart flutter just a little?" he asked in an amused mocking voice.

"Not for a second! Civilization has made me fastidious. They never wash except in sand. It's not their fault I know. Water can only be used for drinking and cooking and watering the animals. It's more valuable than oil."

"Never mind. It was an experience and you will soon be back in familiar surroundings. Do you realize it's taken us all day to drive a few miles!"

"Ten miles on sand seems like a hundred."

They reached Ray as the sun was

setting. Built at the foot of a mountain it was once an ancient capital but now it seemed quiet and lifeless. The town was unawakened behind its earthen walls.

"I read somewhere that every Spring the people in Tehran send their carpets here to be washed with soap and water," Harriet said. "They are spread out on the flat rocks to dry."

"It must look a remarkable sight with all the different colours. We could do with some of that treatment right now. I feel covered in grit," Keane replied. He was looking and feeling extremely weary. Driving on sand was very exhausting. The wheel drag had been a great strain on his hands and wrists.

As they went through the city in the falling dusk both Harriet and Keane felt that they had been away for far longer than the actual two days. One or two people glanced at the Landrover curiously as they drove in at the hospital gates and round to the

Emergency entrance. Two orderlies ran out with a stretcher to carry Morris inside and Keane and Harriet went with them. Keane gave the doctor in charge a brief account of the extent of the injured man's injury and subsequent treatment then took Harriet's arm and led her outside.

"There's no point in you hanging about here. He's in good hands now." He smiled at her kindly. "I expect he will be sent to an intensive care unit so he will be your patient."

Harriet looked up at him gratefully. "I'm so thankful you were with me. I can't thank you enough."

"No need for thanks. I was only too pleased to be of assistance," he said tiredly. "I will see you tomorrow. I'm going to return the Landrover then come back for a bath and a meal. I doubt whether either of us will want to go out tonight."

Harriet left him to walk across to the Staff block. After she reached her room the first thing she did was to turn on the bath taps. It was wonderful to be able to strip off her sand-soiled clothes and step into the hot water. Afterwards she shampooed her hair and stood under the shower to rinse the soap out. Then feeling infinitely better she dressed in clean clothes. When her hair was dry and set she made her way to the dining-room for a meal. She was ravenous for she had not eaten a proper meal since she left the hospital.

She had intended to return to her room and go to bed afterwards but she felt restless. She would never be able to sleep unless she knew that Morris was going to be all right. So she went back to the Emergency unit and found that Morris had already been sent up to her ward.

"He's been cleaned up and X-rayed," the young Iranian doctor told her. "I've only just come on duty. If you want more particulars ask Doctor Maddox."

Knowing no more than she had done before Harriet decided to visit Morris and see for herself. The nurse who was on duty cautioned her before she was allowed to enter the intensive care unit.

"You can only stay a minute or two," she said. "He's become very excitable."

"Is he conscious?" Harriet asked in surprise.

The nurse frowned. "He's delirious. Something is worrying him. I couldn't make any sense of his ramblings. So it could be dangerous to excite him more. Please be very careful."

Harriet smiled to herself for the nurse not having seen her before presumed she was talking to a relative. She will have a shock when she sees me in uniform, Harriet thought. However, she is right to warn me. Morris is in a critical condition.

Morris looked flushed and grabbed Harriet's hand when she spoke to him gently. He had not recognized her for he said wildly:

"Find Harriet. Must find Harriet!" Then he babbled on about papers, important papers which he had to find.

Harriet laid cool fingers on his burning forehead and spoke to him soothingly, "We will do anything you say, my dear. Don't worry. Sleep now. You are safe with me."

There was a screen around the bed so Harriet had not noticed that there was anyone in the room until she heard a man cough in an obvious manner. She started when Keane moved into view.

"I didn't want to embarrass you," he said calmly. "I guessed you thought you were alone."

She stared at him in surprise then said quietly, "Why would I feel awkward? You've heard me talk to Morris before."

He was looking vastly different to the man she had left two hours or so ago. He had bathed and shaved and was wearing a light grey suit and pale blue shirt. His manner was cool, rather remote, his gaze narrow and critical.

"You couldn't stay away, I see," he said coldly. "You ignored my good advice."

She said defensively, "I had to find out how he was. I notice you couldn't keep away."

"That's entirely different. I've been treating him. I ought to be here."

Harriet turned and glanced down at Morris. "Apart from being much cleaner there doesn't appear to be any improvement," she said with a worried frown.

Keane took a few steps nearer to her. "Some fevers are obstinate." He smiled faintly. "Rather like you, Sister. I could understand your impatience if you were still engaged to him. You keep assuring me that it is all over but I'm beginning to wonder."

Harriet's blue eyes became distressed. "I can't disassociate myself altogether. I am worried. I have to admit that. Until I know the extent of the trouble he is in I shall continue to be concerned."

"Hmm! He becomes agitated when

questioned. It's not wise to try to find out what happened to him yet. We know he was shot and that he had nothing with him apart from his clothes. I'm afraid you will have to be patient and wait until the fever has abated."

"It has to some extent. He's not as feverish as when we first saw him." She hesitated then looked him squarely in the face. "Are you going to report it to the police?"

He stared at her silently for a second or two then replied abruptly, "No."

She released a sigh of relief. "Thank you," she said simply.

"There might be questions asked by others," he warned her.

"I know but it will give us a little more time."

"The police may be looking for him."

"Yes. I had thought of that." She stared at him unhappily. "I don't want to get you into trouble. If you think there is a danger of that then you ought to report the accident."

He laughed scornfully. "And have you believe I'm some kind of monster? I would rather risk clashing with the authorities."

Startled by his vehemence she replied quickly, "I would understand."

"No thanks," he said shortly. "I don't care to risk it."

Her blue eyes reflected her uneasiness. "I can't help feeling that it was wrong to bring him here. If he did enter the country illegally he will feel trapped."

"He will have to take that chance," Keane said roughly. "There's no reason why you have to protect him unless . . ." He broke off and grasped her arm. "Harriet, be truthful. Are you hoping for a reconciliation?"

Shaken by his persistence she said unevenly, "Morris was the one who broke it off. I doubt very much whether he would want to try again. I have been honest with you, Keane. I told you it was over for me months ago."

"You are not very convincing." He

released her arm and turned away. "I hope he is worth all the worry and anxiety you are torturing yourself with. I will do all I can. I wish it could be more." He smiled faintly. "You need protecting from yourself, Harriet. You are too softhearted; too forgiving."

She met Stan Maddox as she came from the special care unit. He stopped and gave her a warm, searching glance.

"You managed to get him out then," he said. "Was it very difficult?" Then noticing her look of surprise explained, "I saw him in Casualty and Keane told me a little."

"Yousaf, Nafisa's husband took us to his camp. I would have found it rather awkward on my own. I suppose Keane told you he came with me?"

"Yes." Doctor Maddox frowned. "Why didn't you ask me?"

"I wasn't going to ask anyone. Keane happened to be there when Yousaf gave me a note from Morris."

"Did he say what he was doing in Iran?"

"No. He was unconscious. He didn't recognize me."

"He was in a terrible state; filthy dirty and his wound was badly inflamed."

"I know. We couldn't do much for him at the camp. The conditions were awful." Harriet stared at him with troubled blue eyes. "Do you believe he's going to recover?"

"Why not? He's young and kept himself fit. You saved him in the nick of time. When the fever clears he will recover quickly. Don't lose any sleep over him. I've seen worse cases survive."

"Keane can't understand why I'm so anxious about him."

"That's because he's involved. It irritates him."

Harriet stared at him blankly. "I can't see why. Surely it's natural when you've known someone well."

Stan smiled. "If the positions were reversed you would react in the same manner. You can only see your point of view. One day you will understand."

Harriet frowned. "I feel a little bewildered. Keane behaved in a most unfriendly way just now. I wish you had come with me, Stan. At least I know where I am with you."

"You are both tired and suffering from strain. I think you are making too much of it and misjudging Keane. He has human frailties too, you know," Stan said in a kindly voice.

"Yes. I suppose to an outsider it does seem strange that I can ever forgive Morris."

"Why did he break off the engagement?" Stan asked curiously.

Harriet smiled faintly. "Not because of another woman. I think that might have been easier to understand. He got cold feet and said he didn't want to be tied. He had already applied for a post abroad before he told me two days before the wedding."

Stan gave her a compassionate glance. "You were brave, Harriet. Not many girls would have hidden their grief so well."

"It's over now." Harriet smiled. "Thanks for listening, Stan. You are a very understanding person."

"Any time," he said flippantly. "I have broad shoulders."

Harriet returned to her room feeling much easier in her mind. When Morris recovered she would have no more ties with him. Seeing him again had finally convinced her of her feelings towards him. She no longer loved him.

5

TWO days later Doctor Maddox informed Harriet that Morris could be moved from the special care unit. She had expected this to happen for the fever had gone and he had recognized her.

"I told you he would improve rapidly," Stan said cheerfully. "Keane has paid him several visits but I guess you already know that."

"No, I've missed him each time he's been in. I haven't seem him since we got back."

The doctor glanced at her in surprise. "I had the impression that you were becoming close friends."

"You were mistaken."

"He did offer to take you to the Nomad's camp."

Harriet laughed. "You think he did that to become better acquainted with me? No, it was just a friendly gesture. He would have done the same for anyone."

"You don't know Keane very well then." Stan sent her a quizzical glance. "Just remember I'm here, Harriet. Next time you need a helping hand, ask me."

She smiled, "I'm not expecting another occasion. When shall I move Morris? And is it safe to question him now?"

"Later on this morning and you can ask him anything you want. He's bursting to talk to someone. If he doesn't his temperature will soar." Harriet hurried away to prepare a bed for Morris in a room with three other patients. She was not sure how Morris was fixed financially so did not choose a private room.

She had promised to give an hour of her time to the clinic so that she could help them with the polio vaccines. There had been three cases in the city within the last week and people had been advised to have an injection. The response had been so overwhelming that the clinic had had to ask for assistance.

As things were quiet in her section she decided to go after she had finished with one of the doctor's rounds. Staff Nurse could supervise Morris' removal to his new ward. It would not be wise to single him out for attention. It was nearly lunch time before she got back and was not surprised when her Staff Nurse told her that the patient from the special care unit was asking for her.

"He says he knows you," Staff Nurse said eyeing her dubiously. "He's a very nice looking young man."

"Yes. I am acquainted with him," Harriet smiled. "It was a long time ago. It's just a coincidence that we've met again. If the hospital gossips want to make something out of it please tell them they are wrong."

"Yes, Sister Lawford. I've suffered myself so I know how to deal with them."

"Thank you, Staff Nurse," Harriet said pleasantly. "You might as well go to lunch now."

When the nurse had gone Harriet walked along the corridor to the room where Morris had been placed. His bed had a screen around it and he looked almost as white as the pillows which were propping him up. His hazel eyes brightened when he saw Harriet and he made an attempt to sit up.

"Don't move," she said gently. "You are too weak yet."

He said faintly, "I couldn't believe my good luck when Nafisa told me you were working here."

"You remember writing the note to me?"

He smiled ruefully. "That's about all I do remember. I was in a frightful state." His hand slid out to grasp her hand. "I'm in such a mess, Harriet!"

"There's nothing much wrong with you physically now. If you think I could help then tell me what's bothering you."

"Speak softly! I don't want the others to hear. I haven't anything to identify me, no passport or money. Nothing!"

"I know," she said quietly. "We searched your clothes. What were you doing in the desert? Were you running from the police?"

"Is that what you thought?" He gave her a reproachful look.

"I didn't know what to think. You had a bullet wound. We thought you might have been shot getting across the frontier."

"No. I passed that legitimately. Then I had my passport, money, supplies and a stout truck. It was small but sufficient for my needs."

"Did you take up your post in Saudi Arabia?"

"Yes. I've been at Oman for nine months. Before that I was at Dubai where I lived in a caravan. It's better at Oman. There's quite a village there for employees. A lot of them have their wives and families with them. I've never regretted splitting up with you so much since I've been there. I've missed you Harriet. There were times when I wanted to write to you and ask you to join me."

Harriet said quietly, "You were lonely."

"I was that all right. I didn't write because I hadn't enough nerve after the way I treated you."

"It's over a year ago. I've had time to adjust. You still haven't explained how you came to be in Iran."

"I had a month's leave and I didn't want to go back home. A guy I was working with had taken a trip into Iran and couldn't stop bragging about it so I decided to find out for myself what it was like. I went to Baghdad first then took the road to the frontier into Iran. The weather was perfect and as I was in no hurry I ventured off the main road to Hamadan to see something of Luristan."

Noticing that he was breathing with difficulty Harriet said urgently, "You have talked too much. Rest now. I can come back later."

At that he became agitated and exclaimed fiercely, "For pity's sake, Harriet. I have to explain to someone! To be brief I lost my way in the desert and that night I was attacked and robbed by bandits. They took everything and when I protested they shot me. I don't remember much after that. I expect they left me for dead. I came to in the early hours. My shirt was soaked with blood and I could hardly stand. I've only hazy thoughts about what happened then but I must have staggered about all day in between bouts of unconsciousness. But I do recall the relief I felt when I came across the band of Nomads. They picked me up and carried me into a tent where there were several old women. One of them extracted the bullet." He broke off and grimaced. "I wouldn't care to experience that again! I kept passing out and praying I wouldn't recover. It was ghastly!"

"I can believe that," Harriet said, her

blue eyes distressed.

"Afterwards they brought Nafisa to me because she could speak my language. She told me she had been in hospital in Tehran and spoke enthusiastically about you. My spirits rose then and I summoned up enough energy to write that note."

Harriet was frowning. "If you were robbed we ought to inform the police."

"There's not a hope of getting anything back."

"Now you have told me you can cease worrying about it. I will think of something. All you have to do is get well quickly."

Morris squeezed her hand. "Bless you Harriet! It's been wonderful talking to you again. You got me out of that awful place. I have you to thank for my life."

"I couldn't have done it on my own. Mr Ford Brown is the one you ought to thank."

"The tall man with grey eyes? He's been to see me several times. I didn't know he was there also."

"You can thank him next time you see him. I've allowed you to talk for too long. I do have other patients to see."

"You will come back?"

She smiled. "Naturally. You are on my ward."

His hazel eyes became filled with disappointment. "Is that the only reason?"

She hesitated. Then deciding it would not be wise to upset him said firmly, "Not the only reason. Now do try to get some sleep. You are looking flushed. Doctor Maddox will be annoyed with me for staying so long."

Harriet went away feeling relieved that he was not wanted by the police. She wondered how she could help him and reluctantly came to the conclusion that she would have to ask Keane for advice. His friend at the Embassy might help.

When she met Adina at dinner that evening she asked carelessly, "Does Mr

Ford Brown still go riding with Ailsa, the Austrian nurse?"

The young woman chuckled. "Why ask me? You know him better than I do."

"I haven't seen him lately and you usually know what is going on." Harriet smiled. "I can see I shall have to take you into my confidence. I want to speak to Keane but I don't want to arrange a meeting. I know he goes riding most mornings. If I strolled in the grounds about the same time it wouldn't appear obvious. But if Ailsa is there it might be embarrassing."

"You will be quite safe. She's gone away for a few days."

Harriet looked relieved. "Good, that's one worry less."

Adina glanced at her curiously "Can't you tell me what it's all about?"

"I would rather wait until I've spoken to him. I just want his advice."

"I see and you didn't want him to think you were running after him."

"Something like that." Harriet smiled

ruefully. "It's funny. All the time we were away together I could have said anything to him without feeling awkward. But now there seems to be a huge chasm between us."

Adina grinned. "Be careful, honey. You sound as if you are falling in love. You've become aware of him as a man not just a surgeon you work with."

Harriet's blue eyes looked startled. "Is it that obvious?"

"You've recognized the truth and it's scared you." Adina smiled. "I've come to know you very well Harriet. I've watched it happening. You were interested in him right from that first meeting."

Harriet frowned. "I don't know how I feel. I'm very mixed up. Sometimes he infuriates me. It's not serious."

"I don't believe you."

Harriet laughed uneasily. "All right. Perhaps once or twice I've given him a second thought. But at the moment I have other serious matters on my mind."

Adina raised her slanting eyebrows. "What could be more important than being in love?"

"Do be sensible! I'm not a young probationer with stars in my eyes. I've made one error. I'm not walking into the same trap again."

"It was unkind of me to tease you," Adina said regretfully. "I know how unhappy you have been."

"It's over now. It was kind of you to warn me. Anyway I don't think there is any danger. Keane's not encouraged me. He's been strictly professional."

Adina looked at her thoughtfully but kept her views to herself. She had noticed the way Keane had stared at Harriet when she was preoccupied with something else. It was not the gaze of a man who was disinterested. Keane was a shrewd man. He knew of Harriet's broken engagement. If he was serious he was proceeding cautiously. A wise move in Adina's opinion for Harriet tended to show hardness towards men who tried to be familiar. She was still smarting from the treatment she had received from Morris although she affirmed that she had got over it.

Harriet was sitting on a wooden bench when Keane strode from the hospital dressed in his riding suit. He looked surprised when he saw her but did not hesitate to walk across to her.

"Hello, Harriet! Have you quite recovered from your desert adventure?"

She smiled. "I found it interesting, did you?"

"Some aspects of it." His grey eyes surveyed her keenly. "You don't look very happy. Is something worrying you?"

"Nothing very much. Could you spare a minute to discuss it with me?"

"I guessed correctly, evidently." He moved to her side and sat down. "Out with it! What's bothering you?"

"I've spoken to Morris and I've found out what happened to him."

"Is that all," he said flatly. "I might have known it concerned Morris. I suppose he's in trouble."

"It's not what we thought. He's been working in Oman and was on a vacation. He had hired a truck and intended touring Iran. Unfortunately he was robbed and attacked by bandits. That's how he got shot."

"He's a lucky man." Keane's eyes were quick and intent. "In more ways than one. He's been given a second chance with life and with you."

"I hadn't considered it like that. I suppose it is a strange coincidence."

"If I was in his position I would be having second thoughts."

Harriet smiled. "You wouldn't have behaved as he did."

He stared at her for a few seconds then replied quietly, "Thank you for that, Harriet."

Faint rose colour tinged her cheeks as she met his serious grey eyes. Then hurriedly because she was nervous said, "It's not fair to ask you to help again but you seem the only person. I wondered whether your friend at the Embassy could issue Morris with another passport."

Keane frowned. "I can ask him. Why not come with me? Are you free for a couple of hours?"

"Yes. I'm on late turn today. But I don't want to interfere with your riding."

He shrugged his broad shoulders. "I can do that any day. You will only continue to worry if I don't do something. You will want to get out of your uniform so I might as well phone the Embassy now."

Harriet hurried back to the nurses' block and Keane strolled towards the main entrance of the hospital. When she returned wearing a blue summer dress and white sandals he was waiting for her near the gates.

"It's not far. We can walk there," he told her pleasantly. "I was lucky. Trevor had just returned from lunch. He's offered to give us a few minutes if we come right away."

The Embassy seemed like a fortress in its beautiful, eleven-acre garden with shady trees. Secluded by high walls the main building and adjacent staff residences were mainly Indian in style with sloping roofs and ornamental balconies. Harriet was surprised at its bizarre appearance and even more astonished at the drabness of the offices. In the waiting-room men and women were reading back-dated English newspapers obviously enjoying being reminded of home.

Trevor Palmer was a legation secretary. He was charming, well-dressed and very sure of himself. He came out to greet Keane and Harriet himself explaining that his receptionist had not returned from lunch.

Ushering them into his office he said courteously, "Please sit down. I'm afraid I can only spare you ten minutes."

"Sister Lawford and I are very grateful," Keane replied.

To break the ice Harriet remarked in a friendly voice, "You have one of the best positions in Tehran. However did our Embassy manage to get a building right in the centre?"

The young man smiled. "We used to practically run the country. That's a few years back now but we are reaping the benefit. It's important to have a good location." His amused glance moved on to Keane's grave face. "What's the problem? You look worried."

"You know most of it. A few days ago you lent us a Landrover to rescue a man hurt in the desert."

"I remember. I was told you had returned the vehicle and was expecting you to ring me. Did you find him?"

"I did phone the Embassy but you were out with some trade officials. I intended to come and see you but have been too busy. Yes, we found the man. He had been robbed and shot. He's an Englishman employed by a company in Oman. Harriet recognized him. She had known him in England."

"What was he doing in Iran?"

"He was taking a vacation. He had a

truck, supplies, money and a passport. At the moment he has nothing and is in our hospital recovering from his wound. He will need another passport. We are hoping you will help."

Trevor Palmer nodded. "That won't be too difficult. He won't see his cash or his belongings again."

Harriet said quickly. "He's not too worried about that. It's his passport he is bothered about. Luckily he had arranged to draw money from one of the banks so he did not have too much on him."

"Wise man! I shall have to have a photograph and particulars of the company who employs him. If you and they identify him I can go ahead. It might be a temporary measure but it will serve to get him back to Oman." He pulled out a drawer in his desk and took out a long form. "Ask him to fill in the blank spaces Sister, and return it to me with a photograph as soon as possible."

Harriet smiled her gratitude. "Thank

you so much. It will relieve his mind."

"All in the day's work," Trevor replied smiling back at her. "Now I really will have to end this interview. There's mountains of work and people to see." He glanced at Keane. "Are you coming to our Embassy dinner, Keane?"

"If I can fit it in."

"You can give me the necessary items then. Friday, this week, don't forget! I shall be looking forward to seeing you with your lovely young lady friend of course."

"Ailsa will remind me. She enjoys Embassy dinners."

Harriet left the Embassy with mixed feelings. She was delighted that they had been successful in obtaining help for Morris but Trevor's reference to Ailsa had come as an unpleasant shock. Evidently Keane had been escorting the girl to many such affairs otherwise the young man would not have mentioned her.

"You are very quiet," Keane remarked

looking at her curiously, as they sauntered down Lalezar Avenue gazing at the antique shops. "Are you still worrying over Morris?"

"No. When he has his passport he will be able to return to Oman."

"He may want to stay in Tehran for awhile."

She said unsmilingly, "Why do you say that?"

Keane laughed. "I was only considering what I would do if I were in his shoes. You are here. It would be a chance to patch things up between you."

"Perhaps he will," Harriet replied carelessly. If Trevor had not reminded her of Ailsa she would have told Keane the truth, explain that she no longer cared for Morris. But it seemed more certain than ever now that Keane was attracted to the Austrian nurse and she did not want him to have the vaguest suspicion that the knowledge upset her.

She had lagged behind to stare into a jeweller's shop where turquoise and silver was much in evidence and had to hurry to rejoin Keane who had strolled on ahead. As she was turning into a narrow alley a group of children rushed by. Harriet slipped as she stepped back to get out of the way and caught her arm on a sharp, jutting stone as she fell.

Keane had heard the scuffle and ran back to her. "Are you hurt?" he asked with an anxious frown as he helped her to her feet.

"No, only dazed," she said breathlessly as she dabbed the blood away from the cut on her arm.

He pulled out a clean handkerchief from his back pocket. "This is larger than the scrap you are using," he said. "Here, let me do it."

She felt herself tremble as he tied the linen about her damaged arm and willed herself to hide her agitation. "Thanks," she said shakily. "It's nothing to make a fuss about. It was my own fault." He leaned towards her and brushed his lips against her forehead.

"That's for being a brave girl," he said lightly, his grey eyes amused. Then greatly concerned ejaculated, "For Heaven's sake, what's the matter? You are as white as a sheet!"

She pulled herself away and began to walk on. "I'm all right. I don't want to be back late for duty."

"I will find a taxi."

"No. There's no need, really. I would rather walk."

When they reached the smooth, wider pavement he took her hand and tucked it under his arm. "You are obstinate and foolish. Lean on me," he said firmly.

It was odd how easy it was to obey him. She had forgotten Ailsa momentarily. His nearness was having a strange, weakening effect almost as if she was melting. Vaguely she knew that she would repent of it later but could do nothing to halt the delicious sensation of well-being which stole through her veins.

"That's better," Keane's voice was

deep and amused. "You were as stiff as a poker. I was beginning to believe you disliked me."

She smiled and said quietly, "I seem to make a habit of requiring your help."

"Life hasn't been too good to you, Harriet. I hope the future is more promising."

His words shattered her happy illusion and dwelt heavily on her mind. He was sorry for her. His tenderness and kindness meant nothing more than a sympathetic wish to protect her because he pitied her. Her throat closed up with agonizing pain and involuntarily she withdrew her hand from its comforting resting place. Luckily they had entered the grounds of the hospital and he assumed that it was because she did not want to be seen arm in arm with him.

"I will come to the clinic with you to have that arm dressed," he said.

"There's no need. I can put some plaster on it."

"You might have some dirt in it."

She managed a light laugh. "I'm not one of your patients. I do know what to do."

"Yes, of course."

"I will take a photograph of Morris this afternoon. Then tomorrow I can have it developed."

After a swift glance at his face she knew that she had angered him. His lips had tightened into a grim line and his eyes had darkened.

"I had forgotten Morris." He stared at her bleakly.

She said awkwardly, "I shall have to go in."

"Yes." He hesitated then said gruffly, "I have one of those instant cameras. I can take the photograph for you."

"I've been enough trouble without bothering you to do that."

"It will only take a few minutes. I might as well get all his particulars at the same time."

"Very well. It is good of you. I might not be able to find the time this afternoon."

"I will let you know how I get on," he said curtly and turned away.

Tears were stinging Harriet's eyelids as she stared after him for her disappointment was intense. The exquisite moments had faded into unreality and she was facing the hard facts of her everyday existence. Roughly she brushed her hand over her eyes and resolutely entered the nurses' block and took the lift up to her quarters.

6

HARRIET awoke the next morning with a splitting head-ache. She was not surprised for she had not slept well. She had had to get up in the night to bathe her arm and apply a new dressing for the damage was more serious than she had allowed Keane to know. It was still throbbing when she awoke and she was not sure which was worse, her head or her arm. The thought of the long day ahead did not help. She was due to go on duty at eight o'clock and would not be finished until six.

She felt a little better after she had drunk a cup of tea and took some aspirins and tried not to hurry as she washed and dressed. But she looked very wan and heavy-eyed when she was ready in her uniform. Fortunately she did not meet anyone she knew well at breakfast and was spared having to explain about the bandage on her arm. Talking would only increase the throbbing in her head.

I shall have to see Morris today, she thought as she made her way across to the main block. Sleepy-eyed nurses were going off duty as she arrived and Night Sister greeted her with relief.

"Good of you to be early," she said. "We have had quite a night of it. Three new intakes and a ward of restless patients!"

Harriet nodded. "It's just as well so many are in private cubicles."

Night Sister shook her head. "Sometimes it's more difficult. My nurses have been trotting back and forth all night. Nothing serious, thank goodness but very exhausting."

Harriet who had been glancing at Sister's notes exclaimed, "I notice you have Mr Ainley down for examination. What's wrong with him?"

"Something woke him and he became very agitated. I had to sedate him.

From what I could gather he was upset because you hadn't been in to see him." The Sister glanced at her curiously. "Are you well acquainted with him?"

"I used to know him back home," Harriet said casually. "I will go along and see him as soon as I've given my nurses their instructions."

"I think I've thought of everything," Night Sister sighed. "I will be off. Have a good day!"

Morris gave her a reproachful glance when Harriet entered his small ward. "Why didn't you come yesterday?" he asked disagreeably. "You don't know how awful it is lying here not knowing what is going to happen to me."

She smiled and laid cool fingers on his hot forehead. Then without replying felt his pulse and inspected his progress sheet.

Taking the chair next to the bed she frowned at him and said sternly, "You gave Night Sister a lot of extra work. There's nothing for you to get excited about. You will only make yourself ill."

"There's nothing for me to do except worry! Why didn't you come?"

"Because I went to the Embassy with Mr Ford Brown to ask for a new passport for you. And I was too busy when I came on duty to see you. I do have other patients, you know."

"I'm sorry," he said then more eagerly, "Were you able to get one?"

"Not so fast!" She laughed quietly. "It will take time. Mr Ford Brown is going to take your photograph and a few particulars which the Embassy will need. They will have to get in touch with your company."

"They will co-operate."

"Then you have nothing to worry about. But I'm afraid you've seen the last of your truck and possessions."

"That's the least of my worries," Morris said with a faint sigh. "I have some cash put by, enough to see me through. How long will it be before I have my new passport?"

"It will take a few days at least. I expect it will be ready for you before you leave here."

Morris regarded her curiously. "Why is the man with the grey eyes doing all this for me?"

"I think he feels a little responsible because he saved your life. It's natural for doctors and nurses to take an interest in their patients."

"It wouldn't be because he's in love with you?"

She chuckled. "Mr Ford Brown is one of our best surgeons. We move in different circles."

Morris stared at her moodily. "I envy him. He sees you all the time, I guess. You are very attractive. I bet all the doctors are after you."

"Most of the nurses are nice looking. Not many of them marry doctors. We are here to serve our patients. There's scarcely any time for anything else. I doubt whether Mr Ford Brown notices I'm a woman. I'm merely uniformed assistance."

"I can't believe that." He pushed back his sandy hair from his forehead and asked rather humbly, "If I decide to stay in Tehran for a short time will you let me take you out?"

"If you want to," she said lightly. "When you are quite fit you may feel differently. There are plenty of pretty girls in the capital."

"I've had too much time to think and regret," he said seriously. "I was hoping you hadn't changed, that you might even forgive me."

"I forgave you long ago," she said quietly. "This isn't the time or place to discuss it."

She stood up but he caught her hand as she passed and prevented her from leaving him. Keane chose that moment to appear and his shrewd grey eyes took in the situation immediately.

"Good morning, Ainley," he said suavely. "Sister Lawford is wanted in the main ward so I'm afraid you will have to put up with me for a few minutes."

Harriet hid her embarrassment by moving swiftly away from the bed and going across to the two other patients. She gave them a friendly greeting, examined their progress sheets then went quietly from the room.

She found much to occupy her after that and was supervising the rearrangement of the ward when Keane walked in. Leaving her staff nurse to carry on she moved across to him.

"You look busy," he said smiling faintly.

"Yes. We had become overcrowded so I'm shifting the beds to make more room. Did you want to see me?"

"Walk to the lift with me. You can spare a few minutes I dare say?"

"A nurse can always find time for a specialist," she said.

"You are poking fun. It's good to see you smile, Harriet. You aren't looking very well. Is it your arm? I noticed you had it bandaged."

"I thought it might be more comfortable than plaster. It's not too bad. I had a headache earlier but it has passed now."

"Worrying about Morris?" They had reached the end of the corridor and after he had pressed the button for the lift he turned about and faced her.

"Not now," Harriet told him. "I was pleased we were able to get a passport for him. Have you taken the photograph?"

"Yes and his particulars." He frowned. "Has he been bothering you?"

"No, what makes you ask?"

"When I came across you just now I thought you had been quarrelling."

"You got the wrong impression."

"Really?" He raised a dark eyebrow sardonically. "I suppose I don't have to remind you he's a patient in our care."

"I'm not likely to forget that," she said stiffly.

His eyes narrowed. "I can't make you out. I'm sure you're not as indifferent as you pretend."

"It needn't concern you, Mr

Ford Brown." Harriet regretted her reply as soon as she uttered the words but something in his manner had irritated her.

He stepped back as if she had struck him but his face was as inscrutable as ever when he answered her. "As you say it's not my problem. Good day Sister. I'm sure you have more worthwhile things to do with your time than talking to me."

He stepped forward as the lift came up and Harriet turned away to go back to her nurses. It was not only her head that ached now. Every nerve and bone in her body seemed to be throbbing and she felt strained to breaking point. Why didn't I explain to him? she asked herself in anguished annoyance. It would have been so simple. Instead I had to rebuff him, make him angry. And all because I'm too proud to tell him the truth.

Somehow she got through the rest of the day. She worked mechanically and methodically not allowing herself any time for retrospection. She skipped dinner and went to bed early for she was feeling exhausted after the bad night she had had. And to ensure that she would not wake to re-live the events of the day she took a couple of sleeping tablets, something she rarely did for she did not believe in indulging herself.

When she awoke the next morning she felt much better; relaxed and able to cope with the problem which had been with her ever since she had discovered that she had fallen in love with Keane. Now she could think calmly about it. It had happened and there was nothing she could do to alter it. Life had to continue. Patients were relying on her to care for them and she could only give of her best if she was free from worry.

Every time Keane is kind to me hope springs up to encourage my foolishness, she thought as she went into breakfast. He's never done or said anything to indicate that he thinks more of me than the other sisters and nurses. There has to be a good relationship between doctors and nurses. Successful results depend on team work. If Keane felt the way I do he wouldn't be taking Ailsa out. Look at Stan Maddox! He's never disguised his liking for me. A girl always knows when a man is attracted to her. I've never experienced any such instinct with Keane.

Convinced that she now had her emotions under control Harriet chatted to the other sisters who were taking breakfast. And when she left them to go on duty she felt calmer than she had been for the last few days. Even Morris was unable to upset her when she went in to see him. He greeted her sulkily and became unreasonable making a fuss when she questioned him about his wound which was nearly healed.

"I can't see why I have to stay in bed," he said aggressively. "I feel awful lying here when I'm not ill. Surely I could get up for part of the day?"

Harriet smiled at his sulky face. "It's a sure sign you are getting well when you are grumpy. I will ask Doctor Maddox if you can get up when he does his round. But he doesn't come in until late afternoon."

"Can't you give permission?"

"No I can't. We have to rely on the doctors. Patients often feel well enough in bed. But it's another story when they put a foot outside it. You've been very ill. Your recovery has been remarkably swift. That probably accounts for your irritation."

"I'm not irritable! I've always been fit. I know I'm well enough to get up."

"You lost a great deal of blood and you are still very weak. Be patient a little longer, Morris. It's not much to ask."

"That chap over there doesn't want to get up," Morris said waving a hand at the next bed. "I know for a fact he's okay now. You ought to hear him when there are no doctors around. He says he's enjoying the peace and quiet

184

away from his nagging wife and greedy family."

Harriet smiled. "There's a lesson in that somewhere. He's not fooling anyone. When he's well enough he will be discharged but not before."

"The only thing that compensates for lying here is that I do see you occasionally. But I want more than that. I'm fed up with your pity. I want to do things for you. Make you see I've changed."

Harriet frowned. "I don't pity you. I think you are very lucky. You could have died in that Nomad's camp."

"Now you are reminding me that you saved my life!"

"I told you before that it was Mr Ford Brown who did that. You don't owe either of us anything. If you were fully recovered you would not be talking like this. You would be more rational."

"You think that it's my sick mind that insists I still love you?" Morris asked morosely.

Harriet stared at him thoughtfully. "You ought not to dwell on such things. It was finished between us long ago. And when you leave here you will regret your wild fancies."

"They are not wild or fanciful! I mean every word. It's so darn frustrating not to be able to do anything about it."

"I can't listen to you any longer. In future I shall send my staff nurse in to see you. If I keep away you will soon come to your senses."

"So, I don't mean anything to you now?"

Harriet sighed. "You are being very difficult, Morris. I'm the sister in charge of this floor and I do have many responsibilities."

His face brightened. "Yes, I had forgotten. Naturally you can't talk to me in here. If I thought I had a chance I would be patient. Outside the hospital you can tell me your true feelings. You are not a person to hold a grudge, are you?"

"No. I don't blame you for what you did. It's a long time ago, Morris. I was beginning to forget."

"So I do have a chance! Fate has brought us together again. We've been given a second chance."

"Mr Ford Brown said something like that only he thought that it was you who had been given a break."

Morris stared at her glumly. "He doesn't want you to have another opportunity. He is interested in you himself!"

Harriet smiled wryly. "I didn't finish our engagement. That's what he meant I imagine. There's nothing for me to change my mind about." She stood up. "I'm not talking about it any more, Morris. You are becoming too excitable. Try to relax and I will see if you can get up tomorrow."

She felt a little uneasy after she had left him but she had so many other tasks to perform that she quickly forgot what Morris had said. But later that evening when she remembered she became afraid that Morris was going to create quite a few problems before he went once again out of her life. On that she remained firm. She had no wish to renew their relationship. If she had not known a few weeks ago she understood with certainty now that he was not the man for her. He was just a man she had known and liked before she had understood the real meaning of love. It's very unfortunate that he turned up in this country, she thought in some dismay. I have the awful feeling that he's going to cling. When he's well enough I shall have to tell him the truth bluntly. It might hurt but it will be kinder in the end.

A week passed swiftly. The small jagged wound on her arm had healed and she did not think often of the day she had gone to the Embassy with Keane. She had seen very little of him for he had been kept occupied in Theatre. If it had not been for Doctor Maddox she would not have known what he was doing.

"I can't imagine why you assume that I want to know what Mr Ford Brown is doing," she said one afternoon in a voice tinged with exasperation. "There must be other surgeons performing difficult operations with brilliant technique!"

Stan Maddox grinned. "You're not fooling me, Harriet. Your tiny shell-like ears prick up every time I mention the man."

Harriet chuckled. "You're an idiot! Keane and I haven't said two words to each other for over a week."

"What did you do? You must have said something catastrophic to frighten him off."

"Not a thing. It's all in your imagination."

Doctor Maddox gazed at her thoughtfully as she sorted out the case notes on her desk before handing him those he needed. "It's Morris, it must be!" he ejaculated. "Keane is expecting you two to make it up."

"He will have a long wait then," Harriet said calmly.

Stan glanced at her shrewdly. "Morris seems fairly happy about it."

"I wish you would allow me to run my own life." Harriet's blue eyes glinted with annoyance. "Morris will be leaving shortly and that will be the end of that!"

"I enjoy making you cross, Harriet. You look enchanting."

She laughed unable to withstand his teasing. "You do it deliberately."

Stan gazed at her with a serious expression on his square-jawed face. "Somehow, I have the horrible feeling that you are going to make a mess of your young life Harriet. You would have been far safer if you had settled for me."

She smiled. "I wouldn't have made you happy. Do cease worrying about me. There, that's the lot! You have quite a few to examine today."

"Are you going to the social tonight?" he asked carelessly.

"Yes. I promised Adina I would go with her."

"That's fine. I'm not on call. It's about time we saw you in off duty hours. Lately you've been keeping yourself isolated from the rest of us."

"I know. I'm becoming lazy. It's been rather hectic this last week or two and I've felt too tired to dress and go out."

"Keane mentioned he was going," Stan remarked carelessly.

"Really!" Harriet grinned. "You don't give up, do you? Please start on your round. I have a million things to do. And if you mention Keane's name again I won't give you any tea when you are finished."

"I'm beginning to think I've had a lucky escape," he muttered as he walked along the corridor with her. "Any man who gets you for his wife needs super human qualities."

"You bring it on yourself," Harriet said smilingly.

Morris was up now in the daytime.

He was looking very fit but had returned to his bed for the doctor's round. He smiled at Harriet a little sheepishly when she entered the small ward. Now that he was well he was feeling embarrassed because of the way he had spoken to her. He had made a nuisance of himself and ought to have begged her forgiveness instead of expecting her to care what happened to him.

Harriet had noticed the change in him for some days and was relieved that he was showing some sense at last. Although she had understood why he had acted so unreasonably. When people were ill they often talked irrationally and were ashamed of it afterwards. A wise nurse forgot these lapses and never referred to them.

"I suppose you are ready to spring out of bed the minute the door closes on me," Doctor Maddox said jovially after a swift glance at Morris' chart. "I see no reason why we ought to put up with you any longer. I doubt whether you will ever be as fit as you are at this moment."

Morris grinned. "You need the bed so you want to get rid of me."

The Doctor nodded solemnly. "That's true. We can't have you looking so darn healthy. You will upset my patients. We can't have that. If you are discharged tomorrow have you anywhere to go?"

"One of my pals has flown in from Oman. He's rented a flat for a couple of weeks and has offered to put me up."

"You're not going back right away then?"

Morris cast a swift look at Harriet then said quietly, "No. I'm going to finish my vacation."

"We might see you again then." Doctor Maddox nodded and moved on to the next bed.

Harriet heard Morris mutter her name but she shook her head at him and followed the doctor. This was the patient that Morris had thought well enough to leave. The man had obtained temporary relief from his treatment but damaged kidneys and disorganized liver cells were not easily repaired. The delicate muscle tissue of his heart had degenerated and was gradually being replaced by fibrous tissue.

"Isn't there any hope for him," Harriet asked after she and Doctor Maddox had left the unit.

"He's had two operations. He wouldn't last through another. He knows he will never be well enough to be discharged. The entire circulatory system has depreciated."

"That's why you wanted Morris out of there," Harriet said gravely.

"Yes. Morris isn't the most tactful of men and his rude good health might be irritating to one so ill."

"The man is so brave. He makes light of his condition and he rarely complains."

Doctor Maddox smiled faintly. "It's the not so ill who complain the most. We will see that he does not suffer more than is necessary. Don't look so sad, Harriet. We do our best."

"I know but sometimes it never seems enough."

"Our next patient will cheer you up. It's young Ligozzi the wizard guitarist." Harriet smiled. "He's only nineteen but wonderfully gifted. He speaks five languages!"

"Have you heard him sing?"

"Who hasn't?" Harriet laughed. "I'm forever sending someone in to ask him to make less noise. Italians love opera. I'm sure he's treated us to his complete repertoire."

"Perhaps after this painful episode he will drive more carefully. He was lucky to escape with a fractured arm and broken leg."

Roberto Ligozzi was in high spirits. After greeting them exuberantly he grabbed Harriet with his uninjured hand and kissed her wrist. That over he leaned back and proceeded to give them a lengthy account of his day to day progress. They extricated themselves as quickly as possible but not before he had insisted that they come to his next concert.

"It was fortunate that his fingers weren't damaged," Harriet remarked as they walked on to the next cubicle. "It might have been weeks and weeks before he could play his guitar."

"I'm sure he appreciates that. We're nearly finished, I hope. I can see to the remainder. You go back to your office and pop the kettle on."

"Very well but I expect one of the nurses has done that." Harriet chuckled. "That's one of the things I like about you. You make your round so entertaining."

"Cheeky! I can't think how you ever became a sister!"

Smiling faintly Harriet returned to her office and when Doctor Maddox appeared had the tea made and biscuits set out on the table. "Sorry there are no flowers," she said lightly.

"This is the most enjoyable time of the day," Stan remarked as he sat down and picked up the tea Harriet had poured out for him. "Now you know why I do my round so late in the afternoon." Harriet replied in mock surprise, "I understand it was because the other specialists were senior to you and preferred earlier rounds."

Stan stared at her reproachfully. "You've hurt my feelings. You know how touchy I am about seniority."

"We all have to suffer from that. I can't spend any more time buttering you up. I'm expecting a visit from Sister in Charge of the hospital."

Doctor Maddox swallowed his tea quickly. "In that case I'm off. She's already caught me in here twice. And I can't understand a word she says. If you need me I shall be in Women's Med."

Harriet smiled and sighed with faint relief after he had gone. She was not expecting anyone for half an hour but she had to speed his departure. She was planning to rearrange one or two of the beds in the main ward, those which had not been moved before. She would have to move some of the equipment and that would necessitate sending for an orderly to assist the nurses. She would have to hurry if she wanted it finished in time.

I think some of the male staff imagine sisters spend their day reclining in their offices drinking vast cups of tea and coffee, she thought as she picked up the house phone to ask for an orderly. It might do Stan good to change places with me for a day. He would know then what a multitude of tasks I have to get through in the course of a day.

Harriet had treated herself to a new white dress from her monthly allowance. It had been an extravagance she could not afford but she was tired of wearing the same clothes to the hospital friendly gatherings. Having something new to put on gave the affair an added excitement. White suited her clear skin and golden hair and made her eyes look bluer than ever.

"You look glamorous tonight," Adina remarked smilingly when they met outside the club room. "Are you meeting anyone special?"

Harriet shook her head. "No. I bought this entirely for my own satisfaction. I just couldn't wear that old blue thing again."

"You looked very nice in it."

"It's been seen so many times. It was becoming my off-duty uniform. I don't know how some of the nurses manage to look so smart. I never seem to have much to spend on clothes."

"Some are fortunate like me and rely on their parents to help them out. You need never worry, Harriet. You would look elegant in sackcloth. It's the way you walk and hold yourself. People look at you not your clothes."

"Thanks!" Harriet chuckled. "I shall come to you again Doctor Zeid. You've made my evening!"

"I hope there are some appetizing sandwiches," Adina said as they entered the anteroom where the bar was set up. "I left most of my meal tonight."

"What was wrong with it?"

"Nothing. I didn't feel hungry then. I've been in Theatre all afternoon."

"I understand. I usually feel the same. My word there's a crowd here tonight!"

"Yes. These social gatherings are becoming popular. It's probably because it's cheaper than going out to hotels."

Doctor Maddox and another young doctor beckoned them to join them and they went over to sit at their table. The music was loud and in the main room girls and young men were energetically dancing, careless of the foot-slogging they had done during the day.

"Do you want to dance, Harriet?" Stan asked.

"Not right now. I'm enjoying my drink."

More people were arriving and amongst them she saw the tall, broad-shouldered Keane. The glass in her hand shook and she hastily set it down.

Keane went to the bar, bought a drink then turned round to gaze at the people sitting at the tables. It only took a second or two to discover Harriet's group and he weaved his way across to them.

"Didn't expect to see you here tonight," Stan commented as Keane hooked a chair out with his foot and sat down.

"Why not? I told you I was coming."

"That was before Casualty sent up that emergency. How did it go?"

"The woman will survive." Keane glanced at the other occupants at the table and smiled. "I'm sure no one wants to talk shop. We have enough of that on duty."

Noticing that Harriet had finished her drink Stan stood up and signalled for her to come and dance. Keane's grey eyes followed them as they moved to the next room. Adina who was watching them also, smiled as she saw the glances of admiration cast at Harriet as she passed.

Adina was munching a sandwich when Harriet and Stan returned. Keane asked them if they wanted anything to eat but they shook their heads.

"Another drink then?" Keane did not wait for a reply and disappeared in the crowd about the bar. He returned with a tray of drinks for all of them and was just about to sit down when three more people came in and stood just inside the door.

Harriet was curious to see whom Keane was gazing at and leaned back so that she could see. Her surprise made her start for it was Ailsa accompanied by two men. The young one Harriet recognized for he was a junior doctor. The older man very distinguished with shining, white hair, she had never seen before. Ailsa was looking magnificent in a gold, off the shoulder dress. Jewels sparkled around her slender neck and a white velvet coat or cloak was draped carelessly across her back and arms as if she had slipped it off because she was too warm.

"Excuse me!" Keane said abruptly pushing the tray to the middle of the table. Then without looking at any of them he left to walk across to Ailsa and the two men.

Conscious that she was staring at him in amazement Harriet quickly brought her attention back to her friends. But her hand shook a little as she took the drinks off the tray. Luckily no one noticed for they were all gazing at Keane.

"Ailsa looks as if she's been visiting royalty," Adina said softly. "Did you see her ring?"

Harriet nodded. "I noticed it flashing. That's what caught my attention. It looked like sapphire and diamonds."

"Huge, wasn't it? The rumours I've heard are true then."

"I've not been told anything." Harriet said lightly in an attempt to hide her disappointment at Keane's desertion.

"According to the grape-vine Ailsa isn't coming back. She's left to get married. But no one seems to know who the lucky man is. Keane is high on the list."

"That figures," Harriet said quietly. "They have been seen together frequently."

Stan's friend asked her to dance and when she returned from the dance floor she flicked a swift glance at the bar to see if Keane and Ailsa were still there. The young man had disappeared and Keane was deep in conversation with the older man and Ailsa. A few minutes later all three moved towards the door and left.

That's that then, Harriet told herself unhappily. Keane never sent me a glance before he went. He was so wrapped up in Ailsa and her companion. She smiled wryly. It would have been strange if he hadn't been completely engrossed if he and Ailsa have become engaged.

Stan was giving her a worried frown and when she looked at him said gruffly, "It appears I've been barking up the wrong tree. Sorry, Harriet, for being such a dumb wit."

"Lucky for you I didn't take you seriously," she replied lightly in a brave attempt to cover up how shaken she really was.

But she had not fooled Doctor Maddox and for the rest of the evening he kept close to her side. Harriet was grateful to him although nothing he could do would dull the pain that Keane had inflicted on her that evening. It had been a bitter shock to have her fears confirmed so conclusively and this time she did not believe the wound would ever heal.

7

MORRIS was to be discharged from hospital the next day. His friend from the company in Oman came to collect him and was introduced to Harriet. He was a few years older than Morris and she guessed that he would be sensible enough to restrain his young friend from doing anything too strenuous for awhile.

"When is your next half-day?" Morris asked Harriet eagerly.

"Next Tuesday," she replied a little reluctantly.

"Will you promise to meet me? We can do some sight-seeing and have dinner together." Aware that she was hesitating he added seriously, "I promise to behave. I only want to repay your kindness."

Won over by his humble request

Harriet smiled and nodded her head. "Very well. Shall I meet you somewhere?"

"I will wait for you outside the hospital."

After they had gone she wondered whether she had been wise. But he would have been hurt if she had refused and she did not want to part bad friends. The bitterness between them was forgotten and it seemed silly to avoid him.

Ailsa had not returned to the hospital so it looked as if the grape-vine had been right. Keane also was absent and the Theatre Sister who had been working with him told Adina and Harriet that he was taking a few days off.

"I believe he's gone to Austria," she said in a chatty manner. "He was talking about Vienna so I imagine he's gone there."

"That's where Ailsa lives," Adina said.

"You've heard then?" Sister Haller

asked in her guttural German voice. "We've been expecting it. Ailsa has been at such pains to keep her good news from us but she couldn't hide her excitement. We knew she was going about with Ford Brown and she's not mentioned anyone else. She was afraid that she might be moved to another hospital, I suppose. That's why they kept it quiet."

Perhaps it was fortunate for Harriet that they had a few emergencies that day in Men's Medical. It was tiring and worrying but it did stop her thinking of Keane and Ailsa. She offered to work later than usual so that she could give Night Sister a hand with a serious case which was baffling the specialist and Doctor Maddox. So she felt exhausted by the time she left to walk across to the nurses' quarters.

No one except Adina and perhaps Stan had guessed how upset Harriet had been with the news of the engagement. It was becoming stale gossip now and the grape-vine was busy with more recent happenings. Adina was tactful and kind and tried not to leave Harriet on her own too much. Harriet wished that no one knew. She was fighting a grim battle within herself and even Adina's pity hurt. Each day it became harder especially when she noticed Stan's concern or Adina's compassionate eyes.

She took to strolling about the city on her own whenever she could escape from Adina. Somehow mingling with people who did not know her sedated the pain that was with her constantly. She even welcomed the date she had made with Morris. He was so full of the things he had done since he had seen her that he never thought to question her about her own life.

"Tehran is such an exciting city. There is so much to see and do," he exclaimed as they strolled through the Bazaar. "Pat took me to a House of Strength, Zourkhane, it's called, where athletes practise with Indian Clubs."

Harriet gazed at him in alarm. "I

hope you're not overtaxing yourself!"

"No. Pat keeps an eye on me. Don't you think I look fit?"

"As a matter of fact you do. I can see you've been outdoors a lot. You've lost the hospital pallor."

"You look pale, Harriet. Are you tired?"

"A little. Could we stop at a tea house?"

"Why not. We can go to the Fiamma."

"It's expensive!" she warned him.

He grinned confidently. "The company have given me an advance so I'm in funds. Come on! It's not far. Afterwards we can take a taxi and drive to a theatre."

It seemed a long afternoon and evening to Harriet. The play at the theatre was lengthy and as most of it was in Farsi she found it difficult to understand. Morris, careless as usual, had thought it would be performed in English. Too late he realized his mistake. They both became bored and sleepy and left before the end. Harriet was relieved when he hired a taxi to take her back. Outside the hospital gates Morris urged her to see him again but she refused to make any definite plans.

"You can always phone me," she said. "I'm too tired now to arrange anything."

Disappointed Morris left her to walk back to his friend's apartment. Harriet thinking that she ought not to have gone out with him, trudged wearily through the grounds to the nurses' block. It couldn't have been much fun for him either, she thought. All I did was listen and not very enthusiastically. Somehow I can't enjoy anything these days.

Two more days passed and Harriet became convinced that she would never see Keane again. He had been gone for over a week now and it looked as if he had decided to stay in Vienna with Ailsa. If she wasn't returning then it seemed logical to assume that Keane wouldn't either. Why didn't I think of that before? Harriet asked herself unhappily. I've been counting every day. He might have said farewell before he went! she thought twisting the knife in her wound. I can't mean a thing to him.

Each morning her first awakening thought had been that she might see him that day. Now even that had gone. I feel as if all the incentive has vanished from my life, she mused despairingly. I never dreamed it was going to happen to me again. And this time it's much worse.

When she went into breakfast one morning much later than usual Adina glanced at her in vague alarm. There were dark smudges under her lovely eyes and her face was pale and drawn. Adina watched her toy with the food then push it aside and reluctantly made up her mind to say something.

"You will be ill if you don't eat," she said kindly.

"I don't feel hungry." Harriet smiled

faintly. "There's no need to regard me like that. I know I'm not looking my best."

"I wish I could help."

"No one can." Harriet glanced at her apologetically. "Sorry I've been such a dead weight lately. I hate myself for being so depressed. You must be fed up with me."

Adina shook her head. "You haven't been so bad, quieter perhaps but that's understandable. It was a shock. You might feel easier in your mind after you have seen him and talked to him."

"I don't think he is coming back."

"He will have to unless he's got out of his contract. Ailsa was due to leave soon but Keane hasn't been here long."

"I hadn't considered that." Harriet's eyes brightened for a second or two then darkened as she reflected. "He may have terminated his contract."

"Not many do and he would have to have a good reason. I don't think marriage would be enough. But he is a brilliant surgeon. Something else may have cropped up. I wouldn't think about it, Harriet."

"I try not to think at all." Harriet finished her coffee and got to her feet. "It's the second time in my life that I've been thankful that I have other people to care for. None of us belong to ourselves."

She had a busy morning. It was visiting day and the wards and private rooms had to be neat and tidy by three o'clock. Harriet had never relished the hours when patients had friends and relations visit them. However she did understand how important it was to them and no one could have guessed how anxious she was to keep her nurses from being too harassed. They were rushed off their feet trying to get their tasks finished earlier and after the visitors had left they had to pacify the patients who had become noisy and restless.

There were compensations of course. Harriet was able to see and talk with many of the close relatives of her patients who often came to her for advice. She liked to think that she was helping to reassure the timid and worried ones and was never brusque not even when one or two behaved unreasonably. She was compassionate and kind and made it a practice to put herself in their places before she answered their questions.

That particular day was more hectic than most. In the middle of the morning a man who had been transferred from the surgical ward began to complain of stomach pains. A sudden haemorrhage convinced Harriet that he would have to be sent back to Theatre. She had the bed screened off and after a session with one of the surgeons arranged for the man to be sent to Theatre. Harriet went with him as her staff nurse was occupied and spoke encouragingly to him as he was wheeled from the lift and along the corridor to surgery. By the time they reached Theatre the man was dozy from his pre-medication and

Harriet was able to withdraw her hand from the man's tight hold.

As they passed through the swing doors she gasped in shocked surprise. Two surgeons in gowns and masks were standing close together examining X-ray plates. One of them she recognized instantly. It was Keane. The last person she had expected to see!

A Theatre nurse came over and took charge of the man on the stretcher. "Mr Emanuel is ready for him," she said brightly. "He's scrubbing up. You can leave him with me."

Harriet, very conscious of Keane, saw him turn round to look at her but she did not stay to see if he would come across to her. With a few muttered words to an astonished orderly she hurried back through the swing doors and down the corridor to the lift. Her heart was pounding so much that she was certain it could be heard by others. But no one paid much attention to her. Two doctors and a nurse went into the lift after her and did not notice her extreme pallor or her agitation.

By the time she had returned to Men's Medical she had recovered enough to cast a methodical eye on the whereabouts of her nurses. Two of them were checking the linen and she told them to hurry before she continued up the corridor to the main ward. After inspecting the state of the beds there she glanced at her fob watch. Somewhat surprised for it was nearly two o'clock, she called a junior nurse over to her.

"Clear the trolleys away, Nurse James. Where is Staff Nurse?"

"Mr Bore rang and she went along to his room, Sister."

"I see. Have the screens taken away from the two end beds. Doctor Maddox is making his round early today. I want the ward to be ready before he comes so that there's no panic just before visiting time. And remember, only two visitors per patient!"

"Yes, Sister." Nurse James hurried away on very tired feet for she had been rushing to and fro ever since serving the lunches.

I shall be relieved when Men's Surgical have enough beds to take all their own patients, Harriet thought. A Medical Ward is supposed to be easier to run. But ever since I've been in charge it's been rough going. Casualty send us patients who ought to be in Surgical and we've had a constant stream of men who need post-operative care. No wonder Night Sister is complaining. There's never enough nurses to see to them all. I suppose when I'm due to take over Men's Surgical it will be the other way round. Men's Medical will be overflowing and have to send their patients there.

She sighed philosophically. It keeps us on our toes and so far we've managed fairly well. One or two are due for discharge. Perhaps I've been lucky. So far I've not had any of Keane's patients.

Doctor Maddox was in a hurry and

took his round swiftly and efficiently without stopping to chat to his patients. He seemed irritable, unlike himself and when they had finished Harriet asked him what was wrong.

"Overworked and underpaid," he replied with his familiar grin. "Sorry, Harriet. I didn't think it showed. I had to skip lunch as I so often do."

"I didn't have time for it today either."

"They expect too much of us lately. What is needed is another ward and more staff."

"I agree," Harriet said. "I suddenly realized today that we've got far too many surgical cases. This is supposed to be a Medical Ward."

"Then you will be delighted to hear that you are going to have another; one of Keane's this time."

"I thought I was being too optimistic. I don't feel happy about that. I'm always nervous with cardiac cases."

"This one might be tricky. He's to have intensive care. You will have to leave one of your senior nurses with him. Keane will be on call continuously for the next few days."

"Staff Nurse is the only one I could rely on utterly," Harriet replied frowning. "It's too bad! How are we going to manage?"

"Don't grumble at me, Harriet. When you see Keane let him have it. I've enough to contend with as it is."

"I'm sorry, Stan. I suppose you can't stop for tea today?"

"No. I have a couple more wards to see before three o'clock. I might look in later, after the mob has gone. I'm taking a few days off so I won't be seeing you."

Keane came in just before six o'clock. He looked tired and Harriet felt a pang of compassion for him when she noticed the stoop of his shoulders and the strain in his face.

"I guessed you might be finishing about now," he said. "I wanted to have a word with you in private."

Harriet noticed that her Staff Nurse

was hovering near them and beckoned her over. "Take over now, Staff. And see that everything is left tidy for Night Sister."

"Yes, Sister." The nurse glanced curiously at Keane wondering what he wanted with Sister at this hour.

"We can use the duty office," Harriet told Keane. "Night staff won't arrive for another ten minutes." She led the way and when he had closed the door said formally, "Please sit down."

His dark eyebrows drew together as he gave her one of his disconcerting glances. "Why the stiff and unfriendly greeting?" he asked smiling faintly. "I thought you might have missed me."

She replied carelessly without looking at him, "We have been very busy. Time goes so quickly."

"Evidently absence doesn't make the heart grow fonder," he said with a wry twist of his lips. "We all need a little time for our private lives otherwise we might be in danger of turning into automatons."

Relenting a little she asked quietly, "Did you enjoy your vacation?"

He hesitated then with a flicker of a smile in his grey eyes replied, "It was hardly that, but, yes, I did enjoy it. I suppose you heard I went to Vienna?"

She nodded. "When did you arrive back?"

"Last night, very late. Trevor Palmer met us at the airport and drove us here."

She looked surprised. "You had someone with you?"

"A seven-year-old boy. He's in the children's wing at the moment. That's why I wanted to talk to you before you went off duty. He has a rare heart condition and I'm going to operate. Aftercare is going to be extremely important. I've asked permission for you to be in charge of him. You needn't special him yourself but I do want you around."

She said calmly, "Why me? The children's wards have special care units."

He sighed. "You are going to be difficult. What's up, Harriet? You're not the same person I knew before I went away."

She said coolly, "I'm not refusing to help. I'm a little curious that's all. The Sisters in the children's wing are senior to me."

"I'm aware of that. It's nothing to do with seniority. Of all the Sisters I've met here only you have this special attribute which will be needed. If you want me to be more explicit it's because you have a sensitive and loving nature." He smiled crookedly. "I knew that would embarrass you! How sweet you look when you blush, Harriet!"

She stared down at her hands willing herself to control the turmoil of her emotions. His praise had shaken her to the core and she longed to respond naturally. But the thought of Ailsa caused her to become guarded and when she replied her voice was even and without expression.

"If he is my patient naturally I shall

do all I can for him. When are you operating?"

"Tomorrow morning. I can't say when it will be finished."

"I will inform Night Sister. It will give her time to arrange the nurses' duties. I couldn't possibly be here day and night."

His eyes glinted with faint amusement. "I wasn't expecting you to do that. The boy's father will be coming to Tehran in a few days and will stay until the boy is well. I'm telling you so that you won't be surprised when you find him frequenting your ward."

"Isn't his mother coming?"

"She died when the boy was born."

"I see. That's why you are making certain he has a fuss made of him."

"Yes, I knew you would understand. I've watched you tend the seriously ill. I shall rest easy if I know you are with him."

Her blue eyes regarded him thoughtfully. "You know this boy well. He's not just another patient."

"He's my sister's child. He was born in Salzburg. I hadn't seen him since he was four or five. Ulric, that's his father, brought him over to England to visit his grandparents. I met him then."

"Is his condition serious?"

"It would be if nothing was done." He smiled faintly. "I've taken up enough of your time. I expect you want to get off. I hear you've been out enjoying yourself."

"That's news to me." She looked puzzled. "Who told you that?"

"Trevor saw you getting out of a taxi with Morris."

With a wry little twist of her lips she said, "You have your spies everywhere. I went to a theatre one evening."

"Morris decided to stay in Tehran after all. I'm not surprised. He would have been a fool to leave you."

"That's only your opinion," she replied coolly.

Keane's eyes darkened and his mouth tightened in annoyance. "It's hopeless trying to talk to you in this mood. Why are you so unfriendly?"

"I wasn't aware that I was. It's the end of my duty hours and I'm tired. If I haven't been very entertaining, that's too bad. I can hear Sister Gerste. She will be needing this office."

For a fleeting second or two there was such an expression of hopelessness in his grey eyes that Harriet regretted her sharp words. But the moment passed and when she glanced at him again his face was set, his eyes remote. Doubt assailed her and she told herself that she had imagined it. Why would Keane be unhappy or upset? Hadn't he just become engaged!

With a tiny forced smile she went to the door and opened it. He followed and after thrusting the door wide strode swiftly towards the glass doors.

"I didn't know you were still here!" Sister Gerste said, her brown eyes darting curiously at the surgeon's retreating back.

"Mr Ford Brown is sending us one of his patients tomorrow. I will give you all the details later. Nothing outstanding happened today. I've left the usual data. Hope you have a quiet night."

The meeting with Keane had bereft Harriet of most of her remaining energy and she felt weary to the point of exhaustion as she walked across to the nurses' block. A hot meal revived her a little physically but her mind still refused to become less agitated and uneasy.

Now that she had time to consider what Keane had told her she wondered how he had come to meet his nephew again. Was there some connection between Ailsa and the boy or was it just a coincidence? Keane's brother-in-law could have written to him in Tehran and Keane had taken the opportunity to see his nephew when he went home with Ailsa. Yes, it could have happened like that, she thought. Otherwise Keane would have told Ulric to bring the boy to the hospital. He's very worried about him. I hope its not too serious and that surgery will be successful.

A little warmth crept into her heart as she recalled his remarks about herself. It was gratifying to know that he preferred her to the other Sisters, professionally of course. She smiled wryly. Even that crumb helped a little.

When she went on duty the next day she was feeling happier than she had felt in days. Perhaps it was because she was going to do something for Keane, a service which he would appreciate. And with the boy in her care she was certain to see Keane occasionally. The thought was bitter sweet. Seeing him would give both pain and joy. But providing she kept her emotions well under control she would derive much satisfaction from working with him again.

Harriet waited until one of the Specialists had completed his round before she mentioned the new patient to her Staff Nurse. Then she emphasized the importance of their new charge. The intensive care unit was to be scrupulously cleaned and every item of equipment tested thoroughly before it was used.

"Stay with the cleaning woman and see that she does it carefully," she told her Staff Nurse firmly. "Then get an orderly to move in a bed, drips and other equipment. Number six is empty. We can use that. You know what will be needed. You've cared for cardiac patients before. I'm going to relieve you of all duties for you will be required to stay with the boy all day."

Staff Nurse hurried away to carry out the orders she had been given thinking that Sister Lawford was making rather a fuss about a room for a new admittance. But Sister had not been looking at all well lately. She seemed tired, sometimes listless and tended to speak sharply to her nurses. Ever since that young man left the hospital Staff Nurse told herself thoughtfully. Perhaps she's upset and worried. Mr Ford Brown ought not to send his post-operative cases to us. Sister has too much to do. The worry of a normal ward is bad enough but to have surgical cases as well is more than anyone ought to have to cope with.

Harriet wondered whether Doctor Maddox knew anything about Keane's family and decided to ask him when he made his round. But when Doctor Greenlow turned up mid-afternoon she remembered that Stan had told her he was off for a few days. Oh dear, I never wished him a pleasant vacation, she thought guiltily. It was selfish of me. He's been so kind and considerate.

Doctor Greenlow had three students with him and his round took a long time but as he did not accept her offer of tea Harriet saved a few minutes then. She was expecting a call from Theatre at any moment and felt keyed up and anxious. Not that it was noticeable. Harriet always managed to appear calm and alert. Only she knew how nervous she was about the new admission.

But when Theatre phoned and a few minutes later the boy was wheeled in her nerves quietened and she thought only of her patient. Her heart was filled with compassion as he was gently moved from the stretcher to the bed. He looked so young and defenceless, his child's face grey beneath the dark curls.

Keane had come with him keeping a finger on his pulse and he changed over the drip himself. Seeing Harriet's concern he gave her an encouraging smile.

"Surgery was straightforward, no snags. He is going to be all right."

She sighed quietly with relief. "It was a long operation."

"We finished an hour ago. I kept David in Theatre. Wanted to be ready in case of any emergency. He will feel very sick at first."

Harriet nodded. "Is he to have drugs?"

"He will have to be kept under sedation. When he shows signs of consciousness call me. You can find me through switchboard. I won't be leaving the hospital."

"Staff Nurse will special him but I

will keep an eye on him also."

"Thanks, Harriet." The orderlies and the nurse had gone and they were alone with the boy. Keane put a hand on her shoulder and pressed it hard. "I shall rest easy knowing you are with him."

Every nerve in Harriet's slim body was aware of him. Unspoken words hovered between them as their eyes met. Harriet was the first to move away. Calm and poised she went to the boy's bedside then crossed to the window and pulled down the shade.

When she turned back Keane was standing where she had left him. He was smiling and her heart skipped a beat as she caught the tenderness in his eyes.

"Uniform suits you, Harriet. Will you mind giving it up when you marry?"

She flicked a startled glance at him. "I didn't think so, once."

"What about now?"

"I hadn't given it much thought. I shall have to stay until my contract runs out."

"You've forgiven Morris?"

"Yes." Harriet felt awkward and puzzled by his questions and was not sure how to answer him.

"I guessed you would," he said expressionlessly then as he moved away added, "Call me if you are in any doubt about David. I will look in later."

A heavy ache of frustration and failure settled on Harriet as she watched him go. Somehow she had felt so close to him when he had been discussing David. Yet he had gone on a note of coolness leaving her feeling flat and bewildered. I wish he wouldn't ask me personal questions, she thought uneasily. He can't possibly know how much they distress me.

Reluctant to return to the ward she sat down close to the bed and listened to the boy's heavy breathing. His face did not look quite so grey now that the anaesthetic was beginning to wear off. Gently she put his tiny hand beneath the bed-clothes for he had felt very cold when she touched him then forced herself to put Keane out of her mind.

At five o'clock Staff Nurse came in quietly and glanced at her enquiringly. "I can sit with him now, Sister, if you wish."

Harriet sighed and stood up. "I was enjoying being off my feet for a few minutes but I ought to go back to the ward. I haven't started my report for Night Sister."

"It's all quiet in there. Nothing much has happened except that one of the private patients has discharged himself."

"Did you warn him before he left?"

"Yes. I called Doctor Greenlow. He told Senor Boada that he was acting foolishly but the man insisted on going."

"He will be back. He will find it difficult to treat himself at home."

"That's what the doctor said but Senor Boada said he was fed up with being treated as a guinea-pig."

"I can sympathize with him. We have been trying so many treatments. If it was a case of simple anaemia it would be smooth sailing. It all takes time. I do wish patients would show a little understanding. Diseases of the blood are always difficult. We haven't all the answers yet."

"What a darling little boy!" Staff Nurse had approached the bed and was staring down at David. "Is he something to do with Mr Ford Brown? He seemed very concerned about him."

"David is his nephew."

"I see." The nurse looked at her doubtfully. "Why didn't he go to the children's wing? They have plenty of beds."

"We have been asked to look after him."

"Really? That's a feather in our caps, I suppose." Staff Nurse grinned. "That's the trouble with being too good. We always get more than our share of patients."

"Remember what I said, Staff. Call me at once if there's any change."

"Yes, Sister." The girl gave her a

swift curious glance then turned to check the drip before she sat down.

Harriet returned to the main ward to write a lengthy note to Sister Gerste regarding the new admission before she enlightened her about the various changes that had taken place in the ward that day. She knew she would go over it verbally with her but there was always rather a rush when night staff took over and she did not want to forget anything. Sister Gerste was a little excitable and tended to talk a lot. It was difficult to get a word in edgeways sometimes so Harriet often wrote lengthy reports for her. That way there could be no oversights. Sister Gerste was a capable Sister and would read the notes carefully.

David was still unconscious when six o'clock came and Harriet felt reluctant to go. But she did not think that Sister Gerste would approve of her hanging about and after a swift look at the boy Harriet left and took the lift to the ground floor. She was passing the porter's switchboard near the main entrance when she heard her name called and hurried over to see what the man wanted.

"There's a call for you, Sister," the porter told her. "It's external. You can take it in the booth over there."

It was Morris as Harriet had guessed for no one else would make a call from outside. By the time she had picked up the receiver she had made up her mind what to say.

"Can I see you this evening?" Morris asked eagerly.

"No, I'm going to have an early night," she said firmly.

"What's up? Are you annoyed with me?"

"No. I've had a busy day and I'm tired."

"That's a pity. I was hoping you would have dinner with me. I'm leaving Tehran tomorrow. Pat and I are going on to Samarkand."

"It's not as romantic as it sounds," she warned him. "It's not golden it's monotonous. Meshed is six hundred miles."

Morris chuckled. "We're not going too far on it. It's just so that we can say we've been on the road to Samarkand. If we decide to go to Meshed we shall fly."

"Will you be coming back to Tehran?"

"I doubt it. That's why I wanted to see you tonight."

Harriet hesitated then said evenly, "I wouldn't be very good company. Enjoy your trip."

"It's finished then," he said flatly. "You don't want to see me again."

"It wouldn't be any good, Morris. It's best we part amicably, now."

He sighed. "It's only what I deserve but I couldn't prevent myself hoping. It's a pity. It might have worked. I've changed."

"Goodbye, Morris. Give my regards to Pat."

Harriet replaced the receiver and went on her way unmoved. She did not think for one moment that Morris

238

was breaking his heart over her. Seeing her again had revived some of the romance but it wouldn't have lasted. In a few weeks he will have forgotten me, she told herself with a wry smile. A year ago I would have been so happy to know he still cared. She passed by a flowering oleander bush and went up the steps to the entrance of the staff building. Now it doesn't mean anything to me, she mused. Will I get over Keane as easily, I wonder? No, unfortunately I won't. Keane will always be someone special. For one thing he's never told me he cares for me. He's never let me down. If he made a vow he would keep it.

And that means he will never break his word to Ailsa, she thought, twisting the knife in her heart. The man I love is lost to me forever.

Subdued and unhappy Harriet had little appetite for her evening meal but she pretended to enjoy it because Adina was watching her anxiously. It was good to have friends but being aware that they were worried about her made her plight seem more acute. If only no one knew that Keane was so important to me! she thought despairingly.

Harriet smiled wryly to herself as she sipped black coffee. In a hospital large or small it was well nigh impossible to keep problems to oneself.

8

"I'VE written to David's father and asked him not to come to Tehran for another week," Keane said one morning a few days later.

He and Harriet had just left the boy and were standing in the corridor outside the intensive care unit. Keane was frowning as if displeased, and every movement he made indicated his impatience. Harriet was unable to hide her surprise for it was so unlike him to show any emotion over a patient.

"Is that really necessary?" she asked doubtfully for she had become attached to the small boy who had taken his misfortune at being in hospital so well. "He's such a happy child. He never complains. I can't help feeling that he's very lonely. Surely seeing his father wouldn't harm him."

Keane smiled thinly. "You are

allowing your heart to rule your common sense, Harriet. He has to be kept as quiet as possible. The slightest excitement might prolong his stay here, might even jeopardize his life. The heart tissues have to have time to heal. So far he's responding well. I'm hoping he won't have to have surgery again. The obstruction is no longer there and when the blood vessels are mended he will be as good as new."

"He speaks English like a native. I was surprised."

"Ulric insisted that he had an English Nanny. He thought my sister would have wanted that."

"He sounds a kind and understanding man."

"Yes, he is." Keane seemed reluctant to leave her and Harriet wondered why he was taking his time. Usually he was in such a rush to get back to Theatre. She could only assume that there was not much for him to do there but she was wrong.

"I'm assisting Doctor Hyams with

a suspected gastric ulcer. There's a possibility that it might be more serious than that. Sometimes I feel a great reluctance to enter Theatre. You are such a controlled person, Harriet. It's almost as if you are giving me some of your strength."

"I understand how you feel," she said quietly. "You suspect a malignant growth."

"Yes, possibly. There are times when I wish I had no emotions at all." He sighed. "I shall have to go otherwise they will be buzzing me. There's a film being shown in the Common room tonight. Were you intending to go?"

"No. I have one or two things I want to do," she said quickly.

"Pity. You would have enjoyed it. I won't see you until tomorrow, then." With a frown of disappointment he turned away and walked rapidly down the corridor.

Harriet returned to her ward asking herself why Keane was acting so peculiarly. Whenever he met her these days he seemed on edge as if unsure of himself. He never knew what to say either. At times he was positively tongue-tied with his unspoken words jarring her sensitive nerves. I'm too imaginative, she thought, too keyed up, too aware of him. I suppose it's the contrast. He's always been so confident, never lacking for words, never wasting a minute. Now he tends to stay longer when he visits David. That's perfectly natural for he is his nephew but it's strange because he never stays long at David's side. He makes a point of keeping me outside the unit talking about the most trivial things with long silences in between.

She sighed. It can't be because he wants my company so much. Perhaps he's eager to talk about Ailsa and isn't sure whether I would appreciate that. She smiled twistedly. I certainly wouldn't care to hear him praising her and that's what he would do I imagine. I think in future I shall have to have urgent duties to perform elsewhere when he looks in on David.

A week passed. One of the most rewarding Harriet had experienced in a long time. David was sitting up now and eating normally. Keane had said he could leave the intensive care unit and Harriet was debating where she ought to put the boy. She did not think he ought to be on his own but it would not be wise to place him with the very sick. Then she remembered the young Italian and decided the problem had been solved. Roberto would be an ideal companion for he was gay and amusing. There was only one snag. He had insisted on having a room to himself.

She enlisted Doctor Maddox to help her persuade Roberto and when he was making his round that day mentioned that they had a small boy who was feeling lonely and needed young company.

"He's a brave, happy little boy," she said staring at Roberto intently to see if he was looking at all interested.

"I also am desolate, Sister," he said with a flash of impudence in his dark eyes. "I was longing for you to take pity on me and come and sit with me."

He had caught her hand and was kissing her palm but Harriet stepped back and he had to release her. "If you take pity on David and have him in here with you I might consider it," she said smiling calmly.

"Why not? I agree. But you have to keep to the bargain. If I'm to see you more often I don't care who it is."

Harriet exchanged a smiling glance with Doctor Maddox who remarked casually, "What are all those glamorous females going to say about that? I couldn't fail to notice the queue on visiting days."

Roberto waved his uninjured hand. "Sister is worth all of them," he said extravagantly. "I try to imagine her out of uniform. One day I shall have that opportunity when we go out together. There's so much I can do for her." He cast a baleful look at the room. "This is no place for a goddess!"

Harriet chuckled, "No. I don't think she would last long."

"Lying here with nothing to do has softened your brain, young man," Doctor Maddox said gruffly. "What gives you the impression that Sister would accept any of your invitations?"

Roberto's eyes glinted. "She's a woman, isn't she?"

"Fair enough." The doctor grinned. "If you persuade Sister to go out with you I will give you half my next pay cheque."

Roberto stared at him in mock horror. "It's as difficult as that!"

"It certainly is. I ought to know. My head has frequently been on the block."

"Wrong tactics! It can only be that." Roberto laughed. Then more seriously asked, "When is the boy to come?"

Harriet replied quickly, "After I have Mr Ford Brown's permission."

"I've not met him. What's he like?"

"You are making conversation,"

Harriet told him smilingly. "We have spent far too much time with you."

"No one ever stays long," Roberto said dolefully. "Fractures and broken bones aren't interesting enough."

"I expect he is bored," Doctor Maddox remarked after they had left the Italian. "He has an outsize crush on you. I would be careful Harriet!"

She chuckled. "He's only playful. I bet if I took him seriously he would be frightened to death."

"No he wouldn't. He'd love it. It amazes me how blind you are. You just can't see the damage you cause."

"What nonsense! He has plenty, of lovely visitors. I hope David can move in with him."

"It's very unorthodox. The boy ought to be in the Children's Block. If I had been here I would have put my foot down."

"Mr Ford Brown did get permission."

Stan stared at her thoughtfully. "I suppose you had something to do with

248

it. Keane wanted you to look after his nephew."

"He thought it might be quieter here," she replied calmly.

"Hmm. I can't think what's got into Keane these days. He's like a bear with a sore head. I can't have a rational conversation with him."

"I suppose it's because Ailsa has left."

"He never mentions her. Perhaps they've had a row."

"I doubt it. How could he quarrel with her if he never sees her?"

"It's beyond me. That's enough about Keane. What about you, Harriet? Do you see Morris when you have the time?"

She shook her head. "He's left Tehran."

"Are you going to write to him?"

"I don't think so. It wouldn't be fair to him."

Stan thrust his hands into the pockets of his white coat as they walked towards the lift. "I've got some news for you," he said in a gruff embarrassed voice. "I think I've met the future Mrs Maddox."

Harriet stopped dead and stared at him in astonishment. "Are you kidding?"

"No, I'm not. You might look the tiniest bit upset, Harriet. You're not very kind to my ego."

She gave him a serious, tender glance. "I'm fond enough of you to wish you every happiness. You deserve it, Stan. I mean that seriously. Who is she? Where did you meet?"

"On my last leave at a friend's house. She's English, a secretary in a travel agency. We hit it off right away."

"Blonde or brunette," Harriet asked smilingly.

"Brunette, two years younger than I am. About your height and size with hazel eyes. Anything else you want to know?"

Harriet chuckled. "She's awfully lucky. You will make a marvellous husband."

"Thanks," he retorted dryly. "It's a bit late in the day to hear you say that."

Ignoring his mocking she said quickly, "You did make your mind up quickly."

"A man always knows. It's you women who prevaricate."

"Perhaps we're more cautious."

Stan glanced at her shrewdly. "Pity about Keane. I would have been pleased for you two to hit it off. However if he's chosen Ailsa there's no point in labouring the wish. I was wrong about you both."

Fortunately the lift arrived at that moment and Harriet was able to turn away before he caught a glimpse of her unhappy face. She could not have taken any more of his tactless remarks. However she was genuinely pleased about his good news. He's such a kind man, he really deserves a break, she thought as she walked back along the corridor. I hope his young woman is good enough for him.

She looked in on David and then

went to another private room to check a pneumonia case she was feeling uneasy about. He was breathing with great difficulty and rather alarmed she examined the oxygen and adjusted the tube. Then hurriedly she left him to go to the nearest house phone.

"Sorry, Stan," she said apologetically. "The pneumonia patient is worse. He's more cyanosed than when you saw him."

"Okay. I will be back. Give me a couple of minutes."

Harriet sighed to herself. It meant another nurse would have to be taken off normal duties. I daren't take David's nurse away until I've spoken to Keane, she thought worriedly. He was so definite about not leaving him alone. We shall have to manage somehow. She did not want to ask the Junior to sit with the seriously ill patient. If anything happened the girl might panic, also it wouldn't be fair. Nurse Thomson will have to special him. She's taking the tea trolley around with the Junior. Perhaps one of the patients would help there. They like to make themselves useful when they are allowed up.

"Did you give him the penicillin?" Doctor Maddox asked as he examined the pneumonia case.

"Yes. Staff Nurse administered it ten minutes after you left. She had instructions to examine him at half hourly intervals."

"It was fortunate you looked in on him. He will have to have constant surveillance." The doctor frowned. "I don't like the look of him. If he doesn't become less cyanosed within the next half hour call me."

Harriet smiled faintly. "It's one of those days when I have to be everywhere at once. He is going to recover isn't he?"

"There's nothing more we can do for the moment."

"Sorry. I ought not to have asked." Glancing up Harriet noticed that Nurse Thomson had come quietly into the room. She smiled and said kindly,

"There's no need to be alarmed Nurse. You are to sit with Mr Nelson and on no account leave him alone. If you need more oxygen use the buzzer. I will look in from time to time."

"Yes, Sister," the nurse said quietly.

Harriet followed Doctor Maddox into the corridor and remarked with faint satisfaction, "At least he's in a private room. We didn't have to isolate him. Virus cases are too dangerous to have in the main ward."

"I shall have to get back to my rounds. I've two more to do." Stan smiled. "Be seeing you, I expect."

That didn't sound too optimistic Harriet thought as she hurried back to her office where one of the laboratory assistants was waiting to speak to her. There were a thousand and one things to do before she went off duty and if she had paused to think she would have decided that she would not get through half of them. Yet she managed most of them because her mind was in tune with her work. Fortunately when she paid another visit to Mr Nelson she found that he was less cyanosed and his temperature had dropped slightly. The penicillin was having an effect.

I won't have to call Stan after all, she reflected. That's one anxiety less for all of us. When a patient is dangerously ill it affects the entire ward, patients as well as staff. Having a crisis to deal with had been a successful test for her nurses. Even the Junior had survived on her own for an hour or two without breaking anything or causing a commotion. She was confidently applying new dressings to a patient when Harriet returned to the ward.

Two days later Harriet was astonished to see Keane walking along the corridor with two visitors, a man and a woman. Keane had agreed to have David moved in with Roberto and it was his room he was making for. But when he noticed Harriet he called her over.

"This is David's father, Sister. He is very eager to see his son."

Harriet who had been staring at the

young woman smiled mechanically and said, "David is looking forward to seeing you."

"Ailsa, I think you know," Keane said pleasantly.

"Yes. I have seen her."

Ailsa smiled. She was looking extremely smart in a yellow and white dress and matching jacket. "Our paths never crossed although we worked in the same hospital. I've often seen you, Sister, and Keane has spoken of you."

Worried about her patient Harriet asked, "Does David know he's to have visitors?"

"No. It was wise of you to remind us. Would you see him first, Sister, and give him the good news?" He smiled at Ulric. "He has to be kept as quiet as possible so don't make too much fuss of him."

Harriet went in first and closed the door. Roberto greeted her cheekily but she kept well out of his reach.

"I've come to see David," she said as she moved close to the boy's bed.

"Would you like to have a visitor?"

The boy's brown eyes brightened. "Is it Daddy? Keane said he might come."

"Yes. He's waiting outside. But you have to be very quiet and not get excited. Do you understand that?"

"Yes. Keane explained. I will be good."

"Very well then. He can only stay a few minutes this time so don't get upset when he has to leave."

"I always get upset when you leave," Roberto said saucily making David giggle.

Harriet smiled as she went to the door and opened it. "It's all right," she said. "You can come in."

Keane went into the room with Ulric leaving Ailsa outside. The girl smiled at Harriet who was wondering why she was there.

"I've been told to wait here," Ailsa said. "Keane thinks that two visitors might be too much for David."

"I will send someone with a chair

257

for you," Harriet told her politely and walked on until she came to the linen room. Two nurses were working there and she asked one of them to find a chair and take it to Ailsa.

It looks as if there is a connection somewhere between Ailsa and David, she thought feeling puzzled. If she came to see Keane why come with Ulric? Perhaps they just know one another or they could have travelled on the same plane and got talking. I expect it's very simple, Harriet told herself faintly exasperated. I'm making a mystery over nothing.

But she was to be made still more bewildered when the visit was over. Keane with Ulric and Ailsa in tow came to her outer office and requested a few minutes of her time.

"David's fine," Keane said before she could enquire. "Ailsa and Ulric asked if they could see you before they left. I hope it's not inconvenient."

Harriet glanced up from the forms she had been filling in and shook her head. "No. I expect David was pleased. He has been looking forward to seeing his father."

Ulric smiled at her warmly. "I'm very grateful for the care and attention you have given him, Sister. Keane has told me how kind you have been."

"It was a pleasure. David is a dear little boy."

"I wanted to show my appreciation by giving you something but Keane says it's not allowed."

Ailsa said brightly, "I suggested that we take you out to dinner one evening. We shall be here ten days. You can choose any evening."

Harriet bit her lip hesitantly. She wanted to refuse but with a stretch of nine evenings to choose from how could she do that? She glanced at Keane and saw that he was frowning. Obviously he considered her reluctance ill-mannered.

"Tomorrow evening, then?" she said deciding that it was best to get it over as soon as possible. "It's my half day so it will give, me plenty of time and I won't have to keep you waiting."

"Good! Shall we pick you up here?" Ulric asked with a beaming smile.

Ailsa said in friendly tones, "You needn't wear anything too grand."

As if I could, Harriet thought wryly. Yet it was kind of Ailsa to mention it. I expect she's used to dressing for a theatre or dinner. I would have worried about that not knowing.

Keane was smiling. "We won't keep you, Sister. I guessed you would like to meet Ulric." He turned to the Austrian girl. "Are you, ready, Ailsa? Or do you want to look up old friends?"

"Not right now. We came straight from the airport. I'm looking forward to a bath and a change of clothes."

When the door closed on them Harriet released a quiet sigh of relief and resumed the task she had been doing before they came in. But it was some minutes before she could give the forms all her concentration.

Keane had not said that he would

be going but she presumed he would be there. Engaged couples usually went out together. I wish they hadn't asked me, she thought unhappily. It's going to be extremely awkward and painful.

She often shampooed and set her hair herself but thinking that it would give her more confidence if she had it done by an expert she rang up a local hairdresser and made an appointment for the next afternoon. She made it three o'clock because then she would have plenty of time to return to her room and dress. Ailsa is certain to look stunning so I have to make an effort, she told herself unwilling to confess to herself that she did not want the girl to outshine her. Not that it matters, really, she reflected gloomily. Keane won't notice me if Ailsa is there and Ulric is a man I won't see again after David is well enough to leave. At the rate he is improving that won't be long.

The hairdresser complimented her profusely and asked if he could try a new style. "If you allow me to pin it up it would give you added height," he said. "It's a beautiful colour and the texture is just right."

"No. Just set it in loose waves so that it falls to my shoulders," she said carelessly. "I'm a nurse and I have to pin it up every day. It will make a change to see some of it."

The man was delighted with the result and so would Harriet have been if she had not been so uneasy about the outcome of the evening. She had told herself that she was not going to be nervous but as she dressed and the time flew by she became increasingly agitated.

I don't look on edge, she thought as she stared at her reflection in the mirror. That's my training, I guess. I've learned to keep my emotions out of sight.

She had put on her new white dress and hoped that Keane and Ailsa would not remember it. She doubted that they would for they had taken very little notice of her at the social. Her eyes looked darker than usual and she decided to use very little mascara. Tears might spring to my eyes and I would look such a mess, she thought. They are not very far from the surface right now and the slightest thing could cause a flood. How awful if I burst into tears right in the middle of the meal! It would be disastrous. Not at all in keeping with the way a Hospital Sister ought to behave. But we all have human weaknesses and mine right now is my love for Keane.

A jacket or coat was out of the question. Nothing she possessed was smart enough. I shall have to go without, she decided, already fed up with the idea of going out to dine. It's a warm evening.

Harriet smiled to herself as she picked up her white handbag. All this fuss about my clothes, she exclaimed out loud. I'm really being very foolish.

At five minutes to seven she left her room and walked slowly across the corridor to the lift. Slowly because her heart was beating too fast and her legs were seemingly weak and unco-operative.

When she entered the lobby and saw that Keane was alone her face whitened and she felt herself tremble. Immediately he caught sight of her he strode across to her and took both her hands.

"How lovely you look, Harriet!" he said with a note of admiration in his deep voice.

"Thank you," she replied lightly as she pulled her hands away from his grasp. "Am I too early? Are the others waiting outside?"

"No." He hesitated then took her arm and propelled her towards the door. "We can't talk here. Wait until we are outside."

Standing in the evening sunshine and glancing about her Harriet asked in surprised tones, "Where are Ailsa and Ulric?"

"I have a confession to make," he

said awkwardly. "I asked them not to come. They will make another date with you."

"Why did you do that?" she asked in bewilderment.

"I wanted to have you to myself this evening."

She stared up at him with astonishment in her blue eyes. "I don't understand," she said nervously. "Wasn't Ailsa annoyed?"

"No. She will go somewhere with Ulric."

"But isn't she jealous? Didn't she think it odd? I know I would be upset if my fiancé said he was going to take another girl out for the evening."

Keane smiled. "Ailsa doesn't care about me. She's engaged to Ulric." His eyes narrowed as he noticed her flushed, embarrassed face. "Is that what you have been thinking? That Ailsa was my fiancée?"

"I'm awfully sorry. Everyone thinks the same. I ought not to have listened to the gossip."

He said in exasperation, "That accounts for it! I couldn't make you out. You've been keeping me at arms length for weeks." He broke off to stare at her doubtfully. "Was that the reason or was it because of Morris?"

She laughed shakily. "Morris has gone. I won't be seeing him again."

"Are you sorry about that?"

"No. I'm not interested in Morris."

Two students passed on their way to the gates and Keane took Harriet's arm and pulled her off the path on to the grass. They walked silently side by side until they found a bench beneath a flowering tree.

"No one will disturb us here," Keane said after they had seated themselves. "There's so much I want to say to you. Sometimes I've thought it would be wiser to wait but I've been so afraid that the gulf between us might become too wide. Stan told me that you were so hurt over your broken engagement that it might take years before you would allow yourself to fall in love again."

266

"So much has happened. It was a long time ago. I feel differently now," Harriet said without looking at him. "When I met Morris again I knew I no longer loved him."

"Does that mean that there is some hope for me?" Keane turned towards her and took her hands then went on hoarsely, "Harriet, I have to know! The suspense is driving me mad. I love you so much. I can't stop thinking about you. Every morning I wake up and wonder about you. I'm obsessed with the fear that I might lose you. For heaven's sake put me out of my misery one way or the other. If it's someone else tell me! Perhaps it's Stan. I know he's nuts about you."

"Not any more. He's met someone else."

"Has that made you miserable? You have been looking very unhappy lately. It's worried me so much. But I was afraid to question you." He broke off to smile grimly. "Not that you ever gave me the opportunity. You've spoken so coldly and avoided me. Don't think I didn't notice! Sometimes you made me furious with all your excuses."

"You never guessed why I behaved in that way?" She smiled tremulously. "It was because I felt the same way about you! Keane, I love you. That's why Morris didn't mean anything to me and that's why I was afraid to act naturally towards you."

He was staring at her with such stupefaction on his lean face that she exclaimed, "It's true, Keane. I really love you. It's not infatuation."

She went into his arms as if she never wanted to leave them and raised her head for his kisses with breathless anticipation. Keane groaned and crushed her against him, caressing not only her lips but her closed eyelids and forehead.

"Darling Harriet," he murmured against her golden hair. "Why didn't you tell me?"

She drew back and gazed at him with loving mischief in her blue eyes. "How was I to know you wouldn't have been very embarrassed? I thought you were fond of Ailsa."

He smiled. "I shall have to explain about her." Tucking her hand beneath his arm and holding her close he went on, "I met her nine years ago at my sister's wedding. She was about fifteen then. I never realized whom she was until I ran into her here. We got talking and she told me that she was a second cousin to Ulric. Naturally I was interested for she was able to give me news of David. I was alarmed when she told me that the boy had been very ill and I wrote to Ulric to ask him to bring David to Tehran so that I could examine him."

"So that's why you saw Ailsa so frequently! The gossips thought that it was because you were attracted to her."

"There was only one who interested me and that was you. Anyway I knew she was in love with Ulric."

"Why didn't he send David to you?"

"I imagine it was in deference to Ailsa's father. You see he's a G.P. and David was his patient. When Ailsa went home she explained about my work to her father. He was interested but doubtful and decided to pay me a visit."

"He was the man with Ailsa at the social!"

"Correct! That's why I left you to join them. You were with Stan so I thought you would be looked after. After hearing what I had to say, Ailsa's father suggested that I went back with them to Vienna and see David before any plans were made."

Harriet sighed. "Such a simple explanation and I've been torturing myself imagining all kinds of things. If only we could put the clock back!"

Keane laughed and kissed her. "No. I couldn't stand that. I've had too many despairing moments believing that you had forgiven Morris. Whenever I saw you two together I decided I hadn't a chance."

Harriet asked curiously, "Do you mind about Ulric marrying again?"

"No. Why do you think that? David needs a mother and he is fond of her already. I'm sure my sister would approve. It was so tragic losing her in childbirth. But she was never very strong. I think David takes after her."

"I expect your parents were dreadfully upset."

"Yes. They write to Ulric and David always hoping that they will go and see them. So far it hasn't happened often because of David's delicate health. With David well again they will be able to go very soon."

Keane smiled at her tenderly and Harriet raised his hand to her lips. "I'm so happy for you," she said softly.

"I know so little about you," he said. "Stan told me you had lost your parents. Have you any relatives at all?"

"One aunt in England. The others are abroad."

"I admire your courage, Harriet. It

couldn't have been easy. You will never be alone now. I can fight your battles for you."

She chuckled. "There aren't many left."

He looked at her seriously. "Will there be one when I ask you to give up nursing?"

She shook her head. "It's a profession I can always return to if I have to but right now all I want to do is look after you."

He laughed. "Not as a patient, I hope!"

"That's up to you," she said demurely.

"I suppose we shall have to finish our terms here. I don't know about you but I don't want to wait that long. We could find an apartment, marry and settle down in Tehran until it is time for us to leave. What do you say?"

"It sounds marvellous but I shall need a little time to buy a few clothes. You won't expect your bride to have such a fine selection as Ailsa has, I hope."

His grey eyes twinkled. "It is you I want not your clothes!" He laughed. "You do blush easily, Sister Lawford! What have I said to bring such entrancing colour to your face?"

"It's not what you say, it's how you say it," she replied smilingly. "There's been a few inquisitive people gazing at us. Don't you think we ought to move?"

"Yes, I suppose we ought to. We will hire a taxi and have him drive round and round the city. It's about the only way we shall find any privacy."

Her blue eyes sparkled. "We shall become dizzy!"

"I'm that already. I never dreamed the evening would turn out so well. Would you rather go for a meal and then on to a theatre?"

"I don't care." She smiled. "Anywhere so long as I'm with you."

Harriet had the strange sensation of floating on clouds as they made their way to the gates. It would not last she knew but underlying the exultation was a deep, wonderful feeling of confidence in the man beside her, and a certainty that this time it was right.

THE END

WITH SOMEBODY ELSE
Theresa Charles

Rosamond sets off for Cornwall with Hugo to meet his family, blissfully unaware of the shocks in store for her.

A SUMMER FOR STRANGERS
Claire Hamilton

Because she had lost her job, her flat and she had no money, Tabitha agreed to pose as Adam's future wife although she believed the scheme to be deceitful and cruel.

VILLA OF SINGING WATER
Angela Petron

The disquieting incidents that occurred at the Vatican and the Colosseum did not trouble Jan at first, but then they became increasingly unpleasant and alarming.

DOCTOR NAPIER'S NURSE
Pauline Ash

When cousins Midge and Derry are entered as probationer nurses on the same day but at different hospitals they agree to exchange identities.

A GIRL LIKE JULIE
Louise Ellis

Caroline absolutely adored Hugh Barrington, but then Julie Crane came into their lives. Julie was the kind of girl who attracts men without even trying.

COUNTRY DOCTOR
Paula Lindsay

When Evan Richmond bought a practice in a remote country village he did not realise that a casual encounter would lead to the loss of his heart.

ENCORE
Helga Moray

Craig and Janet realise that their true happiness lies with each other, but it is only under traumatic circumstances that they can be reunited.

NICOLETTE
Ivy Preston

When Grant Alston came back into her life, Nicolette was faced with a dilemma. Should she follow the path of duty or the path of love?

THE GOLDEN PUMA
Margaret Way

Catherine's time was spent looking after her father's Queensland farm. But what life was there without David, who wasn't interested in her?

HOSPITAL BY THE LAKE
Anne Durham

Nurse Marguerite Ingleby was always ready to become personally involved with her patients, to the despair of Brian Field, the Senior Surgical Registrar, who loved her.

VALLEY OF CONFLICT
David Farrell

Isolated in a hostel in the French Alps, Ann Russell sees her fiancé being seduced by a young girl. Then comes the avalanche that imperils their lives.

NURSE'S CHOICE
Peggy Gaddis

A proposal of marriage from the incredibly handsome and wealthy Reagan was enough to upset any girl — and Brooke Martin was no exception.

A DANGEROUS MAN
Anne Goring

Photographer Polly Burton was on safari in Mombasa when she met enigmatic Leon Hammond. But unpredictability was the name of the game where Leon was concerned.

PRECIOUS INHERITANCE
Joan Moules

Karen's new life working for an authoress took her from Sussex to a foreign airstrip and a kidnapping; to a real life adventure as gripping as any in the books she typed.

VISION OF LOVE
Grace Richmond

When Kathy takes over the rundown country kennels she finds Alec Stinton, a local vet, very helpful. But their friendship arouses bitter jealousy and a tragedy seems inevitable.

CRUSADING NURSE
Jane Converse

It was handsome Dr. Corbett who opened Nurse Susan Leighton's eyes and who set her off on a lonely crusade against some powerful enemies and a shattering struggle against the man she loved.

WILD ENCHANTMENT
Christina Green

Rowan's agreeable new boss had a dream of creating a famous perfume using her precious Silverstar, but Rowan's plans were very different.

DESERT ROMANCE
Irene Ord

Sally agrees to take her sister Pam's place as La Chartreuse the dancer, but she finds out there is more to it than dyeing her hair red and looking like her sister.

HEART OF ICE
Marie Sidney

How was January to know that not only would the warmth of the Swiss people thaw out her frozen heart, but that she too would play her part in helping someone to live again?

LUCKY IN LOVE
Margaret Wood

Companion-secretary to wealthy gambler Laura Duxford, who lived in Monaco, seemed to Melanie a fabulous job. Especially as Melanie had already lost her heart to Laura's son, Julian.

NURSE TO PRINCESS JASMINE
Lilian Woodward

Nick's surgeon brother, Tom, performs an operation on an Arabian princess, and she invites Tom, Nick and his fiance to Omander, where a web of deceit and intrigue closes about them.